"Trust me," he said. "I'm an expert on working too much."

River looked down at her, only inches away. "You can ignore your needs, push them aside...but they don't go away. They build up inside of you. Eventually, you have to let off the pressure or you'll do something stupid."

Morgan's gaze didn't move from his own. Instead, she put a hand on his chest and her lips parted softly in invitation. "Something stupid like this?" she asked with an arched brow.

"Morgan..." His breath caught in his throat as he said her name. If she was just flirting, she was playing a dangerous game. He wanted her. If she didn't want him, she needed to step away.

She didn't. She pulled his head down until their lips met. It was an explosive kiss, the contact igniting the fire inside of River that he'd fought to keep down. Any reservations he might have had about tasting Morgan again fizzled away as she bit his bottom lip and he groaned aloud.

She'd gotten feistier than he remembered her to be. He liked that. A lot.

He'd been telling the truth when he said he knew what it was like to work too much and deny himself. He was an expert at that. But he couldn't deny himself any longer. Not when it came to Morgan.

* * *

From Riches to Redemption is the second book in the Switched! duet from Andrea Laurence.

Dear Reader,

In *From Mistake to Millions*, you met Jade, who discovers that she was switched at birth and should've grown up the heiress to a fortune. Sounds like a dream come true, right? Well, this book is the other side of the coin. What if you found out that none of it was supposed to be yours? Your pampered lifestyle, the pressures of being the only daughter of a rich and prominent family... It was all a mistake. What if that glamorous life had cost you the only man you'd ever loved?

Morgan Steele grew up in the spotlight, and when she tried to escape from it all and eloped with poor but lovable River Atkinson, she found that her idyllic life had its price. When her family finds out what she's done, her marriage and her romance with River are wiped from the pages of history. Then, ten years later, River shows back up in her life. He's even more handsome than she remembers, and now he's the successful owner of a company she has to work with for the entire summer. They have to collaborate for a good cause, but when the old feelings start to bubble to the surface, the secrets they've kept could ruin everything.

If you enjoy Morgan and River's story, tell me by visiting my website at www.andrealaurence.com, liking my fan page on Facebook or following me on Twitter or Instagram. I'd love to hear from you!

Enjoy,

Andrea

ANDREA LAURENCE

FROM RICHES TO REDEMPTION

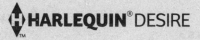

Recycling programs
for this product may
not exist in your area.

ISBN-13: 978-1-335-60384-5

From Riches to Redemption

Copyright © 2019 by Andrea Laurence

Printed in U.S.A.

Andrea Laurence is an award-winning author of contemporary romances filled with seduction and sass. She has been a lover of reading and writing stories since she was young. A dedicated West Coast girl transplanted into the Deep South, she is thrilled to share her special blend of sensuality and dry, sarcastic humor with readers.

Books by Andrea Laurence

Harlequin Desire

Millionaires of Manhattan

What Lies Beneath
More Than He Expected
His Lover's Little Secret
The CEO's Unexpected Child
Little Secrets: Secretly Pregnant
Rags to Riches Baby
One Unforgettable Weekend
The Boyfriend Arrangement

Switched!

From Mistake to Millions
From Riches to Redemption

Visit her Author Profile page at Harlequin.com, or andrealaurence.com, for more titles.

You can find Andrea Laurence on Facebook, along with other Harlequin Desire authors, at Facebook.com/harlequindesireauthors!

One

"Morgan? There's someone I'd like you to meet."

Turning at the sound of her brother Sawyer's voice, Morgan Steele found herself suddenly frozen on the spot. Her eyes were wide and unblinking, her lips trembling but soundless as she stared at the man standing at her brother's side.

She wasn't sure what she had been expecting. Probably just another polite and boring chat with one of her parents' friends and colleagues. Charity fund-raisers for Steele Tools usually meant an endless stream of champagne and small talk with people whose names she wouldn't remember in ten minutes.

Her family hosted events like this at their home all the time. But she knew this man's name. There was no way she would have ever forgotten it.

He'd grown out of his boyish lanky build and into the strong physique of a man who worked with his hands for a living. His closely cropped beard made him look older and more sophisticated than before, but Morgan would know those eyes anywhere. Those navy blue beauties had seen right through her.

"Morgan, this is River Atkinson. He's the owner and CEO of Southern Charm Construction. He'll be working with you this year on our summer housing development project."

Sawyer continued to prattle on, completely oblivious to the reactions of the two people standing with him. At least to Morgan's stunned reaction. For River's part, he actually looked a bit…well…smug. He smiled in a way that told anyone who bothered to look that he was in on the joke. His eyes held a touch of amusement in them as he extended his hand to her.

"It's a pleasure to meet you, Miss Steele," he said.

She knew she should shake his hand. Play along with this ruse and not make a scene. And yet, she couldn't make herself reach out and touch him. That was the same hand that had caressed every inch of her body. The same hand that had slipped a petite diamond ring onto her ring finger during a small rustic mountain ceremony in the Smoky Mountains.

The same hand that had taken a hundred grand from her father and walked away without looking over his shoulder.

"Morgan?"

Her brother's concerned voice snapped her out of her thoughts. She plastered her practiced grin onto her face and thrust her arm out to shake River's hand. She had to treat him like any other business acquaintance. Sawyer didn't know about her past with River. Almost no one did, including all three of her brothers. "It's nice to meet you, too, Mr. Atkinson. I'm sure our companies will do great things together this summer."

His shake was firm, but she could tell that he wasn't interested in immediately letting go of her hand. To be honest, she had a hard time pulling away herself. There was something when they touched—a familiar connection—that lingered there. As though their bodies remembered each other, even if their minds resisted the idea.

Finally, he released her from his grasp. She switched her champagne flute into that hand to let the chilly glass dull the feel of him against her skin. Then she took a large sip to dull the feel of him inside her head as well.

Who the hell had approved this? Her father certainly wasn't involved. He'd just as soon shoot River on the doorstep as let him inside after what happened back in college. But her family was good at keeping secrets, even from each other. It was news to Morgan that Southern Charm Construction and River Atkinson were one and the same entity. She'd heard mention of the company and never once questioned who owned it.

"Sawyer? Can you come here for a minute?" Their mother's voice beckoned one of Morgan's older brothers.

Morgan tensed. She didn't want to be left alone with River. They would hardly be alone in the traditional sense, but being in the same room having a discussion was more intimate than they'd experienced since the day her family pulled them apart.

"If you'll excuse me." Sawyer smiled and clapped River on the back before he departed.

With just the two of them standing on the fringe of the crowd together, Morgan wasn't quite sure what to do. It was more awkward than a junior high dance. What was she supposed to say to the boy—*man*—who had turned his back on her all those years ago?

"You're looking well, Morgan," River said. He was clutching a glass tumbler of scotch in his hand as his dark eyes raked over her from top to bottom. "That emerald dress suits you. It brings out the green in your eyes."

It seemed they were going for polite, but intimate. "Thank you. I like the beard. It makes you look distinguished." It was silly, but she wasn't sure what else to say to him.

River chuckled at her choice of words. "Distinguished. If by that you mean rich and important, then yes, that's exactly the look I was going for." He glanced down at her hand as she held her glass. "Not married yet?" he asked.

Morgan couldn't prevent one dark eyebrow from arching up in surprise and confusion at his question. "Yet? Don't you mean married *again*, River?"

He just shrugged off her challenge with a roll of his eyes. "As far as the state of Tennessee and your family is concerned, you've never been married, Morgan, and neither have I. That's what getting an annulment means. It never happened. That's why you mailed the ring back, remember?"

"Shhh!" Morgan's eyes widened as she looked around at the people nearby to see if anyone was listening. Thankfully, everyone seemed to be involved in their own discussions. She reached out for River's elbow and tugged him with her into a far corner of the ballroom where no one could hear them.

"What is all this about, River?" she hissed at him through clenched teeth.

He crossed his arms over his chest, straining the shoulders of his designer tuxedo. "I don't know what you're talking about."

"The hell you don't. Why are you here tonight?"

"I was invited," he replied with a satisfied smirk.

Morgan sighed in frustration. He was going to make her spell this out just because he could. "How did our companies end up working together, River? This is the first I've heard of it or it sure as hell wouldn't have been approved. Was this your big idea? To weasel back into the family somehow through your business?"

"Why would I want to be in your family, Morgan? For the few hours I was related to the Steeles, I was treated like dirt. You've always been so arrogant. Acting like somehow everything always revolves around your important family and what people want from you." There was audible venom in his voice. "I didn't want anything from you but your love, Morgan, and your father wouldn't even let me have that."

Morgan watched a flicker of pain dance across his eyes. Yes, he'd been hurt. But he hadn't been abandoned the way she had been. "No, he wouldn't, but you seemed all too happy to settle for a fat check instead."

Her father, Trevor Steele, had tried to reason with her when they got back to Charleston that morning. River wasn't good enough for her. He was only using her to get to her money. Eloping? Without a prenuptial agreement? A background check? That little stunt could've had a disastrous outcome, he had insisted. And the boy she loved had his price. His affections were worth a hundred grand. When her father agreed to River's price, money in hand, River had stopped fighting and let Morgan go.

River stiffened at her words. Perhaps he wasn't very proud of that, either. He narrowed his dark sapphire gaze at her for a moment, and then let his arms fall helplessly to his side. "If that's what you really think of me, it's probably just as well our marriage was erased from history. We never would've made it. You must've known that, though. You didn't seem to mind letting your daddy clean up your mess."

Morgan's jaw dropped, her response stolen from her lips. What was she supposed to say to that? Letting her daddy clean up the mess? Really? What did he know of the mess left behind? He hadn't been there. He had no idea what she had been through over losing him. Over losing *everything*. He'd extorted a load of money from her father and carried on with his life. She'd been left behind to deal with the aftermath.

"Morgan, Dad says it's almost time for us to go on stage and beg for money."

She turned away from River as a wave of relief washed over her. Morgan needed the interruption. Things had escalated quickly with years of words bottled up between them, but now was not the time.

She would say something she regretted if she didn't get away from him right now.

"Do you have your speech ready?" This time it was Sawyer's twin, Finn, coming to fetch her. The identical twins were a year and a half older than she was, both with their father's dark blond hair and golden hazel eyes. She could tell this was Finn because of the dimple in his right cheek. Sawyer's dimple was in his left cheek. She also knew Finn was wearing a bright orange bow tie with his tuxedo to agitate their father. Finn lived to exacerbate Trevor Steele.

"I'll be right there." She turned back to where River was standing with an expectant look on his face. He'd called her arrogant, and the way he looked at her made her want to slap the smug smirk off his face. She'd settle for making him eat his words. "We'll have to continue this conversation later, Mr. Atkinson."

"I look forward to it. I'm certainly not going anywhere," he said.

As Morgan turned and made her way up to the stage to join her family in greeting the guests and donors at their annual charity event, she worried that River meant every word he'd said.

Whether it was a promise or a threat, River Atkinson was suddenly back in her life and he wasn't going anywhere.

* * *

River watched Morgan walk away with a grin on his face. He was pleased. For one thing, he'd gotten under her skin. That was exactly what he'd wanted when he set out tonight. And for two, watching the curve of her ass sway in that satin-and-lace gown as she left was a delicious sight that brought back some very hot memories. Her womanly curves had certainly filled out since he'd seen her last. That would make any man smile. Even a man who had spent years plotting to make her regret the way she'd abused his affections.

Those affections for Morgan were long gone now. Swept under the rug with his other youthful naïveté. He should've known that his romance with a rich little princess wouldn't end well. She had just been stretching her wings, rebelling against the tight reins they'd kept on her as a child. That's what college was for after all. The problem was that they'd both taken it too far. They'd fallen in love.

Even that wouldn't have been the worst thing in the world. Love wasn't permanent. Marriage was another matter. It was legally binding. Or at least he'd thought it was until the Steele family lawyers managed to get their little indiscretion wiped away.

And Morgan had let them do it. That was what hurt the most. When Daddy yelled, she'd fallen in line, throwing away everything they'd planned to-

gether. He'd been left with an empty bed and a con-
solation prize, if you could call it that. Some would
call it hush money. Or a bribe to walk away and not
cause a stink. If there was one thing he'd learned
about the Steele family, it was that they hated a scandal. He probably could've gotten more money from
her father if he'd asked for it. Whatever it took to
make River go away.

But, of course, he hadn't thought to do that. He
hadn't wanted to take the money at all. It felt cheap.
What he wanted was his wife back. He wanted the
future he'd planned with her.

When River realized that wasn't going to happen, he knew he had a choice. He could turn tail and
go home with nothing but his bruised pride, or he
could take the money and make something positive
come out of this whole mess. He supposed Mr. Steele
thought he would blow every penny on cheap beer
and an expensive truck, or whatever he thought poor
white trash liked to do with their money.

The joke was on him. River might've been poor
and lacked all those fancy degrees on his wall, but
he wasn't stupid. He took that money and started his
own construction company. He'd practically grown
up in this business, following his dad around job
sites as soon as he was old enough. With his father's
experience, River's drive and a housing boom just

beginning in Charleston, he'd turned that hundred thousand into a hundred million in cash and assets.

And to keep in touch with his roots, when River made his first million, he bought a six pack of Pabst Blue Ribbon and a tricked out Ford F-250 to celebrate. Couldn't let ol' Trevor down, could he?

The sound of applause roused River from his thoughts. The family was done welcoming the crowd and asking for money. That meant his chance to track down Morgan again had come. Unfortunately, the petite brunette was easily lost in the crowd. He supposed she wasn't too eager to continue their discussion, but like it or not, it was going to happen. It had been festering for ten years now and it needed to be dealt with.

Even then, there wasn't a rush to return to their argument. He had time, so he made his way to the bar for a refresher and enjoyed some of the cold canapés being passed around. They weren't particularly filling, but rich people seemed to like fancy foods that cost a lot yet left a gnawing hunger in their bellies.

"Mr. Atkinson?"

River turned to find an older man with a young blonde on his arm. "Yes?"

"Kent Bradford," he said, thrusting out his free hand to shake with River. "I hear you build some amazing houses."

River smiled. "I'm glad that's the word going around, but I like to think of it as well-built homes my customers love. Are you interested in building a property, Mr. Bradford?"

"Call me Kent. And actually, yes I am. Do you work outside of the Charleston area at all? I've secured some mountain property near Asheville, North Carolina, and I was hoping to build a cabin."

His brow went up. "A cabin?" A cabin wasn't worth the time or energy to travel that far. The man could get a better deal from a local company.

Kent chuckled. "Well, I say cabin, but let's be honest. A five-thousand square foot, three-story house is hardly a cabin. I just want it to have that mountain cabin feel. With all the modern amenities and luxuries, of course."

That was more like it. "I haven't built out there, but I would be happy to discuss it with you." River reached into his breast pocket and pulled out a business card. "Why don't you give me a call next week and we can talk about what you're interested in. I can have my architect draw something up."

"Wonderful." The man accepted the card and slipped it into his pocket. "I'll be calling you." With a smile, the man turned and led the younger blonde over to the dance floor.

Tonight wasn't *all* about confronting Morgan, despite what she might think.

It was also about business. Working with the Steele Tools company on their annual charity project was good PR for him. Just being in this room put him within shouting distance of damn near every millionaire in the state of South Carolina. While he waited to talk to Morgan, he was happy to pick up a few business contacts. These types were always wanting to build a summer home or a new status-symbol mansion to keep up with the Joneses, and that meant business was good for him.

He figured that eventually he would get a chance to talk to Morgan again. The room was only so large and the night had really just begun. But the next thing he knew, one of the twins got back on stage. River knew she had three older brothers, two of whom were identical twins, but he couldn't even begin to be able to tell them apart, especially with them all sporting similar, Mark Twain-esque names.

"Ladies and gentlemen, I'm sorry to say this, but we're going to have to end the event early tonight. We've had a family emergency that we need to tend to. If you would be so kind as to see your way out, we would truly appreciate it. Morgan will be in touch with each of you in the upcoming weeks about your support of this year's Strong as Steele community project. Thank you so much for coming."

And with that, the twin disappeared from the stage.

That was odd. The family had gone to a lot of trouble and expense putting this event together. Tickets to attend weren't exactly cheap, either. There must have been something serious going on if they'd chosen to end it and kick everyone out of the house before they got checks out of everyone.

Looking around, River caught a blur of emerald green as Morgan was ushered across the hall by her mother and a large man he didn't recognize. He looked like the former military type despite his expensive tuxedo. The brothers followed them, and they all disappeared into a far room of the house and didn't come back out.

He loitered for a while, letting the other guests clear out of the valet lot in the hopes that someone might come out. But soon, he found he was one of the only people in the ballroom aside from the catering crew that was busy cleaning up. He finally gave up and called it a night himself. When he found no fewer than four police cars outside the mansion as he left, he got the feeling the family emergency was going to take up the rest of their night. Knowing the Steeles, whatever happened would require major damage control to keep the family from looking bad.

Strolling outside, he handed over his ticket to the valet driver and waited for his truck. A few minutes later, the attendant pulled around front with his sapphire-blue F-250 Lariat Super Duty pickup. River tipped him and climbed in.

This wasn't exactly how he'd expected tonight to end. Things felt awkward and unfinished. They'd only begun their discussion when it came to a quick and premature end. Then again, he didn't really know how he'd wanted it to end, either. Perhaps he'd hoped that the sight of him would cause Morgan to swoon? Or maybe that she would rush into his arms and tell him how wrong she'd been and that she still loved him?

Ha. He pulled away from the Steele mansion with a smirk on his face. That wouldn't happen in a million years. His ego wasn't so large as to think she'd given much thought to him over the last decade. He was the poor, unsuitable boy who wouldn't amount to anything. That wasn't the kind of person who loitered in your thoughts. Her big mistake.

No, odds were that she'd tried to put him and their relationship out of her mind as soon as possible. To pretend it never happened just the way her family wanted her to. She probably wanted to put him out of her mind right now, but it wouldn't be so easy this time. River had seen to that by signing an agreement with a representative from Steele Tools who didn't know who he was. Few people outside of her parents would know their history together and their silence had worked to his advantage. Now he was guaranteed to spend a large chunk of the summer collaborating specifically with the company's community outreach representative—Morgan.

At best, he'd hoped she would spend the upcoming weeks regretting what she'd done to him. But after seeing her tonight, this summer might prove to be more pleasurable than he'd expected. At least for him. He hadn't been sure how his former love would look after all these years apart. When she'd turned to him in that stunning green lace gown, he was almost knocked back off his feet. Her exotic green-gold eyes, the high cheekbones, the skin like flawless porcelain... It was as if hardly a day had passed and yet everything was somehow different. Especially when she looked at him with a mix of horror and surprise distorting her lovely face.

The girl he remembered, his bride, had been the prettiest girl he'd ever seen in his life. With her long, luscious dark hair, insightful eyes that saw through his defenses and a sweet-as-sugar smile, he was smitten the moment he'd lain eyes on her. She was older now, perhaps harder, judging by the guarded way she had spoken to him. But even so, he was tempted to fall into her same trap again. Thankfully, he knew better now. Her love came with strings. Baggage. It might come easily, but it could go just as fast.

If Morgan wanted him this time, it was only because he'd achieved his goal and was finally worthy of Daddy's approval. Nothing had really changed about him as a person. He just had money and prestige. Those things were paramount to Mr. Steele. And to Morgan, River supposed.

Hitting the button on his console to open the gate, River slowed at the entrance to his property on Kiawah Island. When it was finally open, he passed down the lane to the home he'd built for himself once he'd finally had the time and money to make exactly what he wanted. A lot had changed since that awful night all those years ago.

River had taken the older man's advice along with his check, walking away and making something of himself with that money. Not to prove anything to Morgan or her father. More to prove it to himself. And he had, many times over. He wasn't the dumb kid he'd been back then. And now it was time for Morgan and Trevor to see how much the man's investment in River had grown. Maybe, just maybe, they might regret judging someone so harshly in the future.

But even if they didn't, he wasn't interested in getting anyone's endorsement these days. Especially from a controlling bastard like Trevor Steele.

Two

"I have the report ready from the fund-raiser. Accounting just brought it to me."

Morgan looked up from her computer to see her assistant, Vanessa, coming into her office with a manila folder in her hand. "That was quicker than I expected."

Vanessa handed over the file. "I'll let you know when your next appointment arrives," she said before slipping back out to her desk.

Morgan opened the folder and her brows lifted in surprise as she saw the bottom line. Given that the event had run for less than a third of its usually scheduled time, she hadn't expected them to raise as much money. They'd never even gotten around to the silent auctions. The family hardly had time to circulate through the crowd and stir up donations. She'd already been planning a contingency for this year's project, narrowing the scope significantly. Considering she had to work with Southern Charm, a part of her would've been okay with cancelling it entirely.

Instead, they'd actually raised more. Apparently, cancelling an event for television-worthy drama in their family made their guests and donors feel bad. And when rich people felt bad, they tended to write a check to feel better again.

Actually, they'd raised enough to build at least three houses in the community this year. And that was just in the month since the event. More funds could still roll in during the next few weeks. Last year, they'd only raised enough for two houses and that had been their all-time high.

That was one bright spot in the dark drama that had plagued her recently. Finding out she had been switched at birth was a major revelation. The news had just come to light and yet, if you asked Morgan, it felt like years since she found out the truth. That sort of news could shift your whole perception of the world. Especially when you realized that your whole life was a mistake.

Normally, time flew by. She lived a pretty busy

life, pouring almost all her energy into the family company and its continued success. When she wasn't at the office, she was at the gym trying to work off the stress and the extra pounds that clung to her hips. She'd always longed for the naturally slender figure of her mother, but instead, her weight was just another item on a list of things that weighed heavily—pun intended—on her mind. But even then, nothing could have prepared her for everything that had happened in her life since that night.

Now, Morgan couldn't even look in the mirror without seeing some imposter looking back at her. How could she have been so blind all these years to the things that were plainly visible to anyone who bothered to look? There was no way she was a Steele. She'd always had a different appearance from the rest of her family—the dark one among a sea of blonds—but it had never registered in her mind what that really meant before the truth came out.

Now she wondered what her parents had really thought all those years. Had her father believed Morgan was the child of an affair with a dark-haired man? Had they thought a recessive gene had come through? They certainly hadn't guessed their real baby girl had been switched with an imposter in the maternity ward or she wouldn't be almost thirty with the last name Steele. Her family would've marched back to the hospital and handed over their changeling the minute they suspected something was wrong.

Even after the truth had come out, there wasn't much they could do. At least at first. The news had come in a double whammy on the night of the charity event: not only had she been switched at birth, but also, the real Steele daughter—Jade Nolan—had just been kidnapped from the steps of their mansion. There was no time to process the impact of the realization. All they could do was dig up ten million dollars to pay the ransom demands.

Morgan had never seen her father that shade of sickly pale before. Not even the night he burst into her honeymoon cabin. Then, he'd been furious. The latest news just seemed to make him heartsick. Even so, he sprang into action in true Steele CEO form. The money was paid, Jade was found safe and the kidnappers had disappeared without a trace. That left a sudden silence where everyone was now absorbing what this news really meant.

Morgan still wasn't sure what would come of all this. Her whole life, her whole identity, had been tied up in being Morgan Steele. The perfect daughter. The baby of the family. Spoiled and doted upon by her parents and her older brothers. Rich. Well-educated. Poised. The ideal member of the family to represent the Steele Tools outreach program. That identity wouldn't change overnight, no matter what the DNA tests said. It would take time to come to terms with it all.

In the meantime, she woke up most mornings feeling lost. Who was she, really? Who would she have been if she hadn't been switched in the nursery that day? It was too soon to know all the answers yet, but the time she'd spent with Jade and her parents had been enlightening enough. She certainly wouldn't have gotten a private school education or gone on to study at Georgetown University. She wouldn't have gotten a Mercedes convertible for her sixteenth birthday or a two-month trip through Europe as a high school graduation present. Her real parents couldn't afford all that. Morgan had grown up with every luxury that should've been Jade's to enjoy.

Then again, if they hadn't been switched, then perhaps Morgan would've been free to live her life the way she wanted to. That was one luxury she could never afford, no matter how big her investment portfolio got.

At this point, she supposed she should be happy that her family hadn't turned their backs on her. This had been their chance to wash their hands of her, and they hadn't. Although she had the reputation of being the perfect princess of the family, it certainly wasn't because she was without flaws. She was fairly sure she regularly disappointed her parents in one way or another. Not intentionally, but it still happened.

Seeing Jade with her flawless skin, white-blond hair and big dark eyes—almost a clone of her mother, Patricia Steele—made her feel like even more of a disappointment. She imagined that even bound on the floor of the dirty warehouse where they'd found her, Jade was more like the ideal Steele daughter than Morgan would ever be.

She'd only been able to spend a little time with Arthur and Carolyn Nolan, and only in a group setting, but it made her wonder if she would feel more comfortable with her biological family. Perhaps they would be so happy to spend time with their real daughter that their expectations would be lower. Perhaps they wouldn't care that she wasn't a perfect size two or that she'd eloped in college with a poor boy she'd loved more than anything. Maybe they would've supported her choices instead of erasing them.

Or maybe she was imagining a perfect situation that had never existed and never could have existed. If she'd been raised as Jade Nolan, she probably wouldn't have met River at that bar in Five Points. Her life would've taken a different path. But there was no going back and no sense worrying about things like that.

A chiming sound came from her computer, accompanied by an instant message from her assistant. Miss Steele, your four o'clock appointment is here, she wrote.

Speak of the devil.

Morgan took a deep breath. And then there was *that* situation to deal with. It was a horrible thing to say, but the kidnapping had been a welcome distraction from River and his unexpected appearance. As though she didn't already have enough going on in her life, he had to pop up out of nowhere. In one night—at one party, even—her past had caught up with her in more ways than one.

Now, her ex-husband was sitting just outside her office, ready to talk about how they were going to spend the summer together. She could hardly even imagine how she was going to get through this.

Morgan wanted to back out. She'd build six houses next year to make up for it. But she knew that wouldn't fly. They'd already announced their partnership with Southern Charm Construction. If they didn't go through with it, it would raise questions. Questions no one wanted to answer. Besides, if she made a fuss, her father would get involved and that was the last thing she wanted.

If Trevor Steele had taught her nothing else, it was that a Steele stayed poised and professional at all times—even in the face of scandal or disaster. So that was all she could do.

Send him in, she replied to her assistant's message. Then she locked her computer screen and prepared herself for another argument. There was no way they wouldn't be finishing what they'd started the other night. If they were going to work together, they needed to clear the air once and for all.

The door swung open and standing in the doorway was River. Today, he'd traded in his tuxedo for a navy suit, but it looked just as amazing on him. He'd found an excellent tailor, she'd give him that. The jacket fit his broad shoulders and narrow waist easily. He was still on the lean side, a runner's physique, but even with his coat on, she could tell his upper body was cut. She supposed that working construction could build up those muscles. It made her want to squeeze a bicep and feel it flex beneath her fingertips.

He smiled at her and she felt her resolve start to weaken as heat crept up her neck. It made her wish she'd worn a blouse with a higher neckline. Or that she'd thought to button it up to the throat before he came into her office. Or worn a scarf. At the slightest agitation, be it arousal or embarrassment, her chest and neck would turn a blotchy red. At its worst, her face would follow suit and she'd look like a furious cherry tomato. She hadn't thought about this appointment when she dressed this morning.

Of course, it would help if Morgan didn't think about his muscles. Or his smile. Or his *anything*.

It was too late for that. Instead, all she could do was wave him inside. He shut the door behind him and casually made his way across her office to the desk where she was waiting for him.

When her father had first ordered the furniture for her office, she'd hated it. It was bulky executive furniture that weighed a thousand pounds and was far too dark for her taste. It was perfect for a mahogany row office, but that wasn't the image she wanted to project. Working for charity while sitting at a ten-thousand-dollar desk was tacky.

At the moment, however, she was grateful for it. Having a mountain of wood between the two of them was almost enough to make her feel comfortable in his presence. Almost.

Comfortable or not, it was time to take control of this situation. She might not be a Steele, but she'd been raised like one, and she wasn't going to let River get the upper hand today. She sat up straight at her desk, lacing her fingers together over her leather blotter and crossing her ankles. This was the pose that flipped the switch in her brain to work.

Then she watched River do the opposite. He unbuttoned his jacket and settled into the chair like he was at home on his couch. He made himself comfortable, sitting back and casually crossing his ankle over his knee as though he didn't have a care in the world. Somehow, that didn't seem fair to Morgan.

Time to make him as uncomfortable as she was.

"Before we get started, I have one question for you, Mr. Atkinson."

"Mr. Atkinson is my father," he noted with a sigh. Judging by Morgan's tone, she was ready to finish their little chat from the party. He was glad he was at least in a comfy chair if she was going to lay into him first thing. This could turn into a very long or very short meeting depending on how the next few minutes went. "But ask away."

"What exactly are you doing here?" Her gaze fixed on him with a pointed expression on her face.

"I'm here to talk about building houses for the poor. Isn't that why you're here?" He couldn't help the sarcasm from slipping into his voice. It was one of the only emotions he had left where she was concerned.

She studied his face for a moment. "I'm serious, River. Why did you sign up for this whole thing? If you only bid on this job to get your chance to tell me off, then just walk away now. This charity project is important to me. If you're not genuinely interested in helping the community, I'll find another contractor."

"Oh, I'm very serious," he said. And he meant it. "This project is essential to me and my company's five-year plan."

"So you're just using the Steele name to make a name for yourself."

"I've already made a name for myself and my company, thank you, but I'd be a fool if I didn't use the chance for some good press and free advertising. Hopefully, that will lead to great things in the future for me and my employees. But listen, I am fortunate enough to be in a position to do some good in the community. This was a great opportunity to do that and get the word out about Southern Charm. There's nothing wrong with that. As the force behind this whole effort, Steele Tools does the exact same thing."

"We do it to help others less fortunate."

River watched her expression as she spoke. She really believed what she'd said. "Maybe you do. But your dad and his stockholders go along with it for corporate promotion and tax deductions, I guarantee it."

"So you really just want to give back? Give your company a little boost?" She didn't seem convinced of it as she spoke. "You're telling me that this whole thing isn't just a ruse to see me again?"

River laughed. Louder than he'd intended to. Enough to make Morgan wrinkle her nose up in irritation. That only made him laugh more. She really was full of herself. "I'm sorry to disappoint, but I've been over you a long time, Morgan. If I wanted to see you, there are easier ways than signing my company up for a summer of charity work for zero profits. So no, this isn't about seeing you again."

He couldn't help but notice a painful flicker cross her face for a moment before she pulled herself back together. Was it possible that he'd hurt her feelings? After everything that had happened, he'd wondered if she had cared about him at all. There hadn't been one word, one email, one text after she left him alone in that honeymoon cabin that night. Just an envelope a few days later with a wedding ring inside.

And for that half a second, he saw the face of the girl he'd once loved. The one overflowing with emotions and vulnerabilities. One that would've held out hope that her first love might still carry a torch for her after all these years. Then the poised, ice-cold princess returned.

"Of course, you're over me," she said. "I was thinking more along the lines of you wanting to give me a piece of your mind. Maybe tell my father off?"

"While speaking my piece might be therapeutic,

no, it's not about you, little girl. I didn't even know that I'd be working with you when I started this process," he lied. He couldn't have her thinking otherwise or she might believe she had the upper hand in their situation. He might've been driven here out of revenge or even masochistic curiosity, but it wasn't a pining for Morgan.

"I'm a professional. I couldn't have built my company up from nothing if I wasn't. Besides that," River continued, "you seem to be a hell of a lot more upset with me than I am with you, although I have no idea why."

She straightened in her chair, studying him with obvious disbelief. "Are you serious? You can actually sit there and tell me you have no idea why I would be upset with you?"

"Wait a minute," River said, holding up his hand before she could go any further. "You really are. Why would *you* be upset with *me*?"

That was certainly an unexpected twist on the situation. Especially since he wasn't the one whose family broke up their honeymoon and wiped their marriage from the books. He wasn't the one who dutifully packed up and went home the minute his father snapped his fingers.

"I've got a hundred thousand reasons to be upset with you, River Atkinson."

Ah. *That.* River had known the moment he cashed that check that it would come back to haunt him. That money was tainted. Dirty. And yet, that same money had changed the trajectory of his whole life. He wouldn't apologize for making the best of a shitty situation.

Instead, he smiled. He knew that would get to her. "What's the matter, Morgan? Did you think you were worth more than that? Should I have asked for a million to keep quiet about our indiscretion? I'm sure dear ol' Daddy would've paid anything to get his little princess out of that mess. Tell me, did you panic when you realized the consequences of what we'd done? Did you wait for me to fall asleep that night and call him to come get you?"

"Of course not," she snapped. "I don't even know how he found us, much less how he knew we'd gotten married."

River shook his head. "I'm sure he tracked your cell phone and credit card records, knowing every step you took. You might've thought you were an adult living your own life, but he just let you believe that. Trevor had you on a short leash the whole time." He chuckled to himself and looked around at her well-appointed office. "And now you work for Daddy. He probably invented this whole job just for you. You probably live in one of Daddy's houses and charge up Daddy's credit cards. Sounds to me like he's still got you on that leash."

Morgan's eyes narrowed at him in anger. "You shut your mouth. You don't know anything about the dynamic between my father and me."

"Don't I?" he challenged. "The woman I met at that bar by the university was confident and independent. She wanted to go out into the world and make a difference. The girl who crawled from my bed with her tail between her legs was someone else entirely. Would you care to explain that to me since you think I don't understand what happened on our wedding night?"

Morgan's pale skin flushed with a crimson undertone along her chest, throat and cheeks. It reminded him of his younger blushing bride. And their wedding night where the blush traveled lower than the low *V* neckline of the blue silk blouse she was wearing now. Then her jaw flexed tight to hold in the angry words she probably couldn't wait to spew at him. She looked like she was about to blow.

"My father cares very much about me," she managed to say between tightly gritted teeth as she gripped her collar and held it closed to block out his prying eyes.

"No. *I* cared about you. I loved you. You're just a prop in your father's perfect family presentation.

You have to fall in line or you're cut from the spot-light."

"Not everyone wants to be in the spotlight, River. I would've much rather lived a life of my choice in the shadows than a life crafted for me on my father's stage."

River shook his head. "I don't believe you for a second. At any time, you could've stood up for yourself. You could've stood up for me. For our marriage. But Daddy's money was too important to risk on a future with some poor boy with a little promise but no education. If he'd cut you off, what would life have been like for you? You would've had to really work for a living and make do without servants like the rest of us poor schmucks. Or from what I've heard, the way you would've been raised if you hadn't been switched in the hospital."

River watched the blood drain from her face. He went too far mentioning that whole thing. He'd read about it in the papers, but he was sure she was still working through it all. He shouldn't have let all his emotions out at once. They'd been bottled up for years, festering, with their only outlet being his company and building it to be the best it could possibly be.

"It would've been easier if I hadn't been switched," she said in a voice barely louder than a whisper. "When you have nothing, there's nothing to take away."

"I'd heartily disagree on that point. I've lost plenty." Morgan's green-gold eyes met his for a moment before she looked away uncomfortably. "It may not have seemed like much to you, just a rebellious fling with an unsuitable boy, but it was everything to me."

Morgan sat silently, a frown transforming her face into a guilty expression. Her gaze dropped to the blotter on her desk. "We need to stop this. It isn't going to change the past, so we might as well put it behind us and try to be civil."

"Of course." River pressed his fingertips together thoughtfully. "I wouldn't want to cause a scandal for the Steele family. Again."

"River…" she warned.

"Like I said before, I want this project to be a success. We have some important work ahead of us. So you're right, we can't let our past interfere. Truce?" He arched his brow at her in a challenge. He knew he could behave, but silencing her sharp tongue might prove more difficult.

Morgan breathed a sigh of relief and her practiced smile returned to her face. She seemed confident in her abilities. He almost missed her anger once it was tamped down. At least that was a real emotion.

"Truce," she said and offered her hand across her desk.

Tentatively, River reached out and took it. Instantly a sizzle traveled up his arm and down his spine, exploding in his groin like a shockwave of arousal. He pulled away as quickly as he could and buried his hand beneath the desk to rub the sensation off his palm and onto his pant leg. It had been like that the night of the party, too, making him both eager and cautious about touching her again.

They might be calling a truce on their fight, but the connection between him and Morgan was far from over.

Three

Three days later, her meeting with River still preyed on Morgan's mind. They'd finally started discussing business and made headway on their project together, but it had been hard to get through it. At least for her. She couldn't tell what River was thinking with that smug grin on his face all the time.

Even as he'd smiled, Morgan had felt herself being twisted in knots. He brought out so many different emotions in her, she hardly knew how to feel. The hardest to overcome, however, was the attraction. She was not supposed to be attracted to River any-more. Not after what had happened. Not after what he'd done. And yet, her body and her mind disagreed on that point. She still wanted him. If she closed her eyes, she could feel his hands on her body again. The way she responded to him. The press of his lips against hers.

And it pissed her off.

She hated feeling off balance in her life and lately that's all she was. At the moment, she was sitting in the gardens at her parents' estate, sipping a glass of wine. She should feel at ease. But she was anything but. She was expecting another stressful visitor. This time, it was the woman who had lived her life for thirty years.

The back door of the house opened up and their housekeeper, Lena, stepped out and gestured the petite blonde in Morgan's direction. She made her way down the cobblestone path to the table beneath the vine-covered pergola that offered necessary shade in the oppressive summer heat Charleston was known for.

"Please, have a seat," Morgan said as she approached. "Would you care for some chardonnay? I pulled a bottle from the family wine cellar."

Jade settled into the chair, but she seemed stiff and nervous. "Perhaps that would help," she said. "I'm more anxious about all this than I expected to be."

Morgan smiled and poured her a drink. "It will help. That's why I'm already a glass into this bottle.

I'll ask Lena to bring another and in no time, we'll be completely at ease with this crazy situation we're in."

"Oh, don't go to any trouble."

"It's no trouble. She'll be out with some nibbles in a minute."

Jade frowned and looked over her shoulder. She was uncomfortable with having staff wait on her, Morgan could tell. "Don't think of them as servants. They're household employees, that's all. They're really a necessity to keep the house running smoothly. My mother certainly doesn't have the hours in the day to keep this massive house clean and everyone fed. She's as busy as my father some days and he runs a company. They're a godsend, Lena especially, and I assure you that my father pays them handsomely for what they do for us."

"Really?" Jade asked with wary eyes.

"Oh, yeah. Lena has worked with us since before I was born. She's like family, but I don't think she stays out of loyalty. We make it worth her efforts. And besides that, if any of us kids ever treated her or anyone else around the house like they were lesser than us, we'd get our ears boxed."

"I find that hard to believe."

"Oh, believe it. My brothers have gotten it more than once for sassing the staff. It's a delicate balance being from a family like this. You have every advantage, everything you might ever want, but you're not allowed to act like it. Especially living such public lives as the faces of the company. But my parents won't tolerate that kind of behavior even behind closed doors. We're the same as anyone else."

Unless, of course, that someone else was a poor boy who wanted to love their daughter in a legally binding sense. It was one thing to treat others well. Another to treat them too well.

Lena approached the table a moment later with a silver platter in her hands. On it was a plate of tea sandwiches, some cookies and another bottle of wine. It was already opened and ready to drink.

"Oh, Lena! You read my mind," Morgan said with delight. "I was going to ask you for more wine."

Lena chuckled and placed the platter on the table. "I've known you your whole life, Miss Morgan. There's never just one bottle of wine. You all enjoy. Let me know if you need me to bring anything else." She turned and disappeared as quickly as she'd arrived.

"That would be hard to get used to," Jade said as she watched Lena walk away.

Morgan picked up her wine and took a sip. "You'd be surprised." Even as she said the words, she heard River's voice echo in her mind and frowned.

Daddy's money was too important to risk on a future with some poor boy with a little promise but no education. If he'd cut you off...you would've had to really work for a living and make do without servants like the rest of us poor schmucks.

Perhaps she was more attached to her lifestyle than she'd allowed herself to admit, then and now. She had loved River, but the truth was that she hadn't thought everything through. What would she have done after the honeymoon? When they moved into their cheap apartment and had to cobble together a life with furniture from a thrift store and boxed macaroni and cheese? How long would the love have lasted then?

Thanks to her overbearing father, she'd never know.

"I suppose if someone hadn't plotted against us, I might feel differently," Jade said. "It's hard to imagine my life being like this."

"Isn't your fiancé rich?" Morgan asked. She hadn't spent much time talking to Harley Dalton socially, but the news stories about the kidnapping had mentioned his successful investigations and security company. He'd been able to pay a large chunk of Jade's ransom and was on the trail of her kidnappers—something the police weren't having much success with themselves.

"Yes," Jade said with a large sip of wine. She looked down at her engagement ring as though she still didn't believe a rock like that was on her finger. "I'm still getting used to the idea of that, too.

Fortunately, he's self-made, so he understands that there's an adjustment period. We've been staying at his mother's estate for a few weeks now while he continues the investigation. She has a housekeeper, but I still find myself tidying up before she can get a chance to clean anything. I tried to buy generic granola bars at the store the other day and Harley kept taking it out of the cart and replacing it with the brand-name kind. It's just a different mind-set."

"I feel the same way when I think of how my life was supposed to be. Where would I have ended up, you know?"

Jade nodded solemnly. "The more I think about our situation, the more questions I have. Those are the kind that can never be answered, so I try to focus on the ones that can. Like who did this to us? And why?"

"To be honest, there's a part of me that wants the answers and a part of me that just can't deal with any more drama in my life. I know my father—*er*, our father, *your father*?" She stumbled over what titles she should use with Jade.

"You can just call him your father," Jade said with an understanding smile. "It's easier that way."

Morgan smiled back, noting just how much Jade looked like her mother when she did that. Her pale blond hair and dark eyes were Steele through and through. She didn't have the confidence or the designer wardrobe, but it didn't matter. She was one of them. The rest of those things would come in time.

Morgan tried to suppress a pang of jealousy as she looked over Jade's striking features. Her father had spoiled her mercilessly, but there were a few things in life that Morgan couldn't have. River was obviously one. Looking like her mother was the other. She knew now that she took after Jade's mother, Carolyn, who was an attractive and curvaceous woman, with bright eyes and flowing dark hair. There was nothing wrong with that; it just wasn't the willowy and pale look Morgan had always longed for from a young age.

It made her wonder if she'd be more content with herself, kinder even, if she hadn't grown up in the shadow of the elegant and gorgeous Patricia Steele. Another question that would never be answered.

"Okay, I know *my* father is throwing money at your fiancé to get to the truth and that's fine by me. I would like to know eventually. But I'm leaving all that investigation stuff to the two of you. My summers are wild and all of this couldn't have come up at a worse time for me. As it is, I'm struggling to find the time to see your parents and Dean. I'm sure they think I'm avoiding them, but really, I'm not. Life just never seems to cooperate."

Jade nodded. "I understand. And so do they. I haven't spent much time with them, either, between work and helping Harley with the investigation. I think I have a bit more invested in this whole thing since the kidnapping made it more personal."

"Of course. You were certainly baptized into the Steele family in a dramatic way. My eldest brother, Tom, was kidnapped, too, when he was a baby. Being a Steele comes with its share of benefits and complications. Do you and Harley think your abduction is related to the switch?"

"I don't know how it couldn't be. I've never been a target of crime in my life before I went public about my DNA results. We've just got to get the last pieces in place and hopefully it will all make sense. I'm looking forward to it being settled. I want to know the truth, I want the bad guys behind bars and then I just want to move on with our lives the way they are now. I want to get to know you and my new family. Plan my wedding. You know, focus on normal stuff for a change."

"Normal is just a state of mind. But I understand. We've had a lot of big changes this year and not a lot of time to work through them. Getting to know your parents. And you…" Morgan hesitated. "I don't know what to call you. We're not related in any way, but we share families through an odd twist of fate. It seems like we should be sisters."

"I think that's what we should be. The truth is too complicated to explain to anyone else, and honestly,

I've always wanted a sister. Dean is a great brother, but it's just not the same."

"Yes!" Morgan said with enthusiasm. "Growing up in this house as the youngest with three older brothers?" She groaned aloud. "When I was little, I was desperate for someone to play with that wouldn't rip my Barbie's head off and launch it on a catapult to take out a lineup of enemy toy soldiers."

Jade laughed and picked up her glass of wine, finally seeming to be at ease. "I guess it's decided then. We're officially kin."

Morgan raised her own glass and they brought them together with a satisfying clink.

"Sisters," they said in unison.

Damn. Morgan was looking frustratingly fine today.

It was a surprise, considering that River hadn't been entirely sure Morgan was going to show up. Partially because he hadn't actually spoken to her about this little rendezvous. He'd left her a voice mail when he knew she wouldn't be available to answer. Like a damn coward. They may have called a truce, but he still didn't want to talk to her in person—for an entirely different reason presently.

Now, instead of getting irritated, he'd get all twisted up inside at the sound of her voice. His blood would start rushing in his ears and his thoughts would stray to their honeymoon night. He had been too busy this morning to lose his focus just to talk to her.

It was bad enough how much time he'd already lost to blatant fantasizing where Morgan was concerned. Watching her saunter toward him now in a tight pencil skirt, clingy knit top and stilettos was a memory that was likely going to headline in tonight's thoughts. It made him wonder if she'd intentionally dressed this way to meet him. Just to make him crazy. With the sunset behind her, her outfit highlighted every womanly curve she had like the silhouette of a '50s pinup girl heading his way.

And for that, he was very grateful. Even if it made him awkwardly tense for a few minutes while he got his libido in check. He hadn't really considered this complication when he bid to work with Steele on the project. Now, he realized that being around Morgan all summer would be an extended exercise in self-restraint for him. He'd never been one to deny himself what he wanted, but this was definitely a case where indulging would be a bad idea.

It *was* a bad idea, right?

"Good evening, Mr. Atkinson."

River looked at her with a furrowed brow of irritation. They'd talked about this already, but she seemed to take pleasure in riling him up. Indulging was definitely a bad idea. He got the feeling Morgan would push *all* his buttons, good and bad.

"Good evening, River," she corrected with a wry smile that barely curled the dark plum of her lips. It was a beautiful color that matched the flowers in her skirt and popped against her pale skin.

He wanted to kiss every bit of it off her despite knowing better. "Good evening, Morgan. Thanks for meeting me on such short notice. I thought you would like to see this."

River turned and gestured to the grassy over-grown property just beyond him. It was in an area near downtown Charleston that was gentrifying and property values were slowly going up. He'd gotten a tip on this land before it was even officially listed for sale.

"This lot is three quarters of an acre. Perfect to split into three quarter-acre lots. That's actually pretty spacious this close to downtown. There will be a big enough backyard for each family to run and play. Maybe put up a swing set or a little pool. A patio. A grill. Everything they would need."

"What's the price?"

River turned back to her with a grin. She was going to love this part. In their business discussions, he'd learned quickly that Morgan wanted to help, but she had an ironclad budget to keep to. He supposed that you had to if you were going to help as many people as you could. "It's ten thousand less than the property you showed me in West Ashley when we met the other day."

Morgan's dark eyebrows went up in surprise. "Really?" She turned and glanced around the property to see what was wrong with it. He'd done the same thing when he heard the asking price initially.

"There's nothing to concern you. I've done a full survey already. The owner inherited the property. He's more interested in selling quickly as a single lot than he is in taking the time to divide it up and find individual buyers, even if it means making less money. If we make him a cash offer before he gets a real estate agent involved, he'll probably jump on it."

"How did you even hear about it? It isn't listed. I looked after I got your voice mail."

"Yeah, I know a guy."

"You know a guy? That sounds sketchy."

"It's not, I promise. I just know a few people from my years in the construction business that are always happy to let me know when they hear about a property I might be interested in."

Morgan nodded and glanced back at the land. "If it's really the price you mentioned and it's not an ancient burial ground or a former Superfund site, I say let's put in an offer tomorrow morning. There's no way we'll find anything better for that price. Especially in this area of town."

"Check—no zombie corpses and no toxic waste. We should be good to go. I'll get the offer drawn up in the morning and hopefully we can get closed on this quickly."

"Great."

All this had happened faster than he'd expected, but there wasn't much reason to linger in an overgrown field with her. They turned together and he started walking her back to the white Mercedes convertible she'd driven over. Back in college, she'd driven a similar, older model. Just the sight of it now reminded him of long winding roads with the wind in their hair and not a care in the world. That was a long time ago, though. A simpler time.

"River?" she spoke about halfway to her car, bringing his thoughts back to the present.

"Yes?"

She stopped and turned back to the empty lot. "You know, as a developer, you could take that land for yourself and build some trendy and expensive row houses here. You probably could make a fortune with the way this area is trending up. When that downtown walking trail is done, you could easily get three quarters of a million dollars each. Are you sure you want to use it for this project? We could find a different property. The one in West Ashley

wasn't bad. I could probably get the price down."
Morgan turned to look at him with her question lin-
gering in her eyes.

River shook his head. She was right, but he hadn't
even considered it. "No, that's okay. When I saw
this land, I could see our little houses sitting on it.
Kids running through the sprinklers in their grassy
yards. I saw three families that were proud of their
new homes. The kind that I would've loved to have,
that my mom would've loved to have when we had
nothing. That's what I want. Not a bunch of trendy
three-story pseudo-historic town houses at ridiculous
prices. There's enough of those around town these
days. The whole area is losing its character thanks
to all the HGTV home-flippers."

Morgan studied his face for a moment when he
was done speaking, and then she smiled. He wasn't
sure if he'd said the right thing until that moment.
She might've been more impressed by the take-
charge, make-money answer he hadn't given, but
he'd given the answer she might not have expected
but wanted to hear. Before he could say anything,
she leaned in, gripped the lapels of his suitcoat in
her hands and pressed a sweet, soft kiss to his lips.

River hadn't been expecting that. And yet, the moment her lips touched his, he knew it was everything
he'd been waiting for over the last decade they'd

spent apart. Suddenly, all his worries and cares didn't seem to matter anymore. There was just this moment.

He was finally able to get his stunned body to respond to his brain and brought his hands to rest at her waist. He wanted to do more than that, but he held back. Nothing Morgan had said or done up to this point had indicated she wanted more than a working relationship. This kiss could mean anything. He'd learned long ago not to presume when it came to the female brain and how it worked.

And then, as suddenly as it happened, she pulled away, leaving him confused, aroused and confused. It bore repeating.

He stood looking down at her in stunned silence as she finally released her hold on his jacket and took a step back out of his personal space. Her eyes were glassy and unfocused as she looked at him, even a bit shaky on her feet with those tall heels.

He reached out a hand to catch her elbow and steady her and she smiled. "Thanks."

"What was all that for?" he asked.

Morgan took a deep breath and wrapped her arms across her chest, hugging her sweater tighter to her curves. "When you were talking before, I was just thinking that maybe you're a pretty good guy after all."

"Uh, thanks?" River wasn't quite sure what to say to that. He'd always thought he was a good guy, but apparently Morgan felt otherwise. It was probably the money thing. With her, it always came back to the money thing.

And yet, she'd just kissed him.

Her gaze dropped from his and surveyed the ground for a moment awkwardly. "I probably shouldn't have done that," she said. "It wasn't very professional."

"I didn't mind." He said the words a touch too quickly, making her look back up at him with a soft smile curling her dark lips.

"Still. My father would frown on my behavior. I'm representing the company after all."

"Your father would disapprove of anything that involved me. Honestly, I can't believe he let me through the front door."

Morgan's lips twisted in thought for a moment before she shook her head. "I doubt he knows. Or if he does, he kept his mouth shut about it. My brothers worked the details, I'm pretty sure, and they don't know about…us."

River stuffed his hands into his pockets and rocked back a bit on his heels. "Wow. Your family is really good at keeping secrets. I know your father likes to keep private issues private, but to keep things from each other… That's next-level secret keeping."

Morgan narrowed her gaze at him for a moment and then nodded slowly with a sad expression on her face. "You have no idea."

There was something about the way she said the words that made him wonder if there were more Steele family secrets than just their ill-fated marriage. He wanted to ask but thought better of it. If she felt like sharing, she would tell him. Besides, he imagined there had to be more than a few skeletons in the closets of that big mansion of theirs. Some of those doors were best kept shut.

With a sigh, Morgan's expression shifted back to her usual practiced facade, but when she looked at him, there was a twinkle of mischief in her eyes instead. "You know, this isn't very professional of me, either, but what the hell… Can I buy you a drink?"

Four

The waiter put a glass of wine and a tall pilsner glass on the table between them. River hadn't anticipated ending up in a bar with Morgan tonight, but he wasn't going to complain. He didn't have anything else to do. It was either crash at the small apartment he kept downtown and work, or drive out to his home on Kiawah Island and work. It was the same thing he did every night, typically staying in the city during the week and escaping to his coastal retreat on the weekends. But no matter where he was, not much was going on. Honestly, this day had brought more highlights than the entire month that preceded it.

He tried not to think about how all those high-lights featured Morgan.

"So tell me what you've been up to, River. It's been nearly a decade since my unscheduled departure from your life in the middle of the night. What happened after that?"

Sitting down, having a real conversation with Morgan seemed a bit surreal. They'd gotten past the initial resentment and anger, moved through the polite discussions and now they were getting to the real talk. He was curious to know what she had been doing with her life, too, but his own stories were not that exciting.

"The short answer is that I've been working ever since you left. You remember how I was working construction with my dad back when we were dating?"

Morgan nodded.

"Well, I took the money from your father and started my own construction business. It was what I knew. I'd met plenty of good guys who were willing to come work for me, and with my dad's experience and guidance, I was able to get the company up off the ground. Actually, I worked my tail off, seven days a week, to get where I am today. It's only been in the last year or so that I've been able to take a breath."

"It takes time," she said. "My father inherited a

company that was already very successful, but even then, he was in the office more than he was at home when we were young. Things change. Competitors come and go. The market shifts. Right now, we're coping with losing retail space in brick-and-mortar stores and expanding our online presence. You've got to stay on your toes or you can lose everything you've worked for."

"Don't I know it. And really, starting a construction business right at the tail end of the housing bust was the dumbest thing I could've done. People were foreclosing left and right. But I watched the market and started with small houses that people could actually afford to buy. I worked with a financing company that went through hoops to get people approved when almost no one could get a home loan. It made all the difference. There were times I worried, though. I even started going to college online in the evenings in case I needed a backup plan."

Morgan perked up in her chair. "Really?"

"Yeah. I have an expensive framed diploma on the wall to prove it. I got a degree in industrial management. I'm not sure what I would've done with it, but I never had to find out. That's enough about me. What about you? I presume you finished school, although I never saw you around Columbia *after*."

"When summer was over, I went back to the University of South Carolina and finished the fall semester. I didn't leave campus very much, though. I wasn't doing that well with my classes after everything that had happened, so I was trying to focus and keep my grades up. After that, I decided to take a semester off." Morgan stopped talking to take a large sip of wine. "So I took a break and went home for a while. Then I ended up transferring to Georgetown and finished school there."

"I didn't realize you left South Carolina." River hadn't kept tabs on her, but honestly, he couldn't have even if he'd wanted to. The Steele family left almost no digital footprints to follow. After her father took her away, it was like she'd never even existed. She could've spent the last ten years on the moon for all he knew.

"Oh, yes. I actually still live there most of the year. I have a town house in the Georgetown area that I started renting when I was still in school. I ended up loving the area and stayed. I come to Charleston for the summers to work on the annual charity project, and then I return home. Our company has a large production facility across the river in Virginia and that's where my office is."

"Where do you stay while you're here?"

"At the house." As she said the words, she looked at him and chuckled into her glass. "I know," she said after swallowing some wine. "Living in the same house with my parents is not ideal. They watch me like hawks, always have, but I try to ignore it. I suppose I could get my own place here. I've just always felt like doing that meant I might never leave again. I don't want that tethering me."

River couldn't imagine spending every summer under his parents' roof again. It wasn't like he spent every evening partying with prostitutes or something, but he chafed under the supervision. If he wanted to leave dishes in the sink, or heaven forbid on the coffee table, it was okay. "Do you hate being home that much that you'd rather stay there than commit to some real estate? You wouldn't have to buy. There are short-term rentals you could get. A beach house, even."

"I know. My father insists I stay there with them. For practical reasons, of course."

"Of course," River agreed.

"But you're right," she sighed. "I should find another option."

River lifted his glass and flashed his most charming smile. "Lucky you, I just so happen to know of a couple of amazing properties available in town."

When Jade got home from her shift at the pharmacy, she found her fiancé, Harley, in his mother's formal dining room. She had never returned to her rental bungalow after the break-in. Harley had all her things packed up and they'd taken up temporary residence at his mother's mansion until he was done working the case for St. Francis Hospital.

In the meantime, he had taken over the space as his pseudo-command center for his investigation into her thirty-year-old baby-swapping case. He had boxes of files, his laptop and anything else he could get his hands on sprawled across the large oak table. He was sitting at the head of the table, frowning at his computer screen like an unhappy king at a feast.

"What's wrong?" Jade asked. She put her purse down in one of the dozen ornate wood-and-velvet chairs and circled behind Harley to rub his shoulders. He had always taken this case seriously, but after the break-in at her house and her kidnapping, it had become personal for him. Almost all-consuming. Some nights she had to drag him to bed.

"I can't find the file I'm looking for. I've searched everywhere. It has all the information about the hospital staff that I reviewed with the former CEO."

Jade pressed her fingers into his tense muscles, eliciting a low groan from him. She glanced over his chair to the table and the boxes set out across it. Harley might be an investigator, but he was first and foremost a man. They couldn't find anything, usually because it required moving something else and it wasn't in plain sight.

"When did you see it last?"

"The day I went to his house. It has the personnel files and photos of all the nurses and physicians working when you were born. I've been looking for it since your family went out on the yacht with the Steeles a few weeks ago. I need to find that nurse's information."

With a sigh, Jade walked over to the boxes. It had been a while since her families had had their first get-together. It had gone well enough, but with everything going on, she'd forgotten about Patricia and Carolyn's discussion of the day the girls were born. Thankfully, Harley hadn't. She glanced in a few boxes, flipping through some things before moving to the next one.

"It's not there. I checked twenty times."

Then Jade picked up one of the boxes, revealing the manila folder that had been beneath it. It was marked with a red *confidential* personnel stamp from the hospital. She didn't say a word. That would just irritate him. She simply picked it up and laid it across the keyboard of his laptop.

"Are you serious? Where was it?"

"Doesn't matter. What matters is you have it now. What are you looking for?"

"The nurse Patricia and Carolyn were talking about on the boat. Her name was Nancy Crowley. When I spoke to the former hospital CEO, he mentioned how she'd committed suicide at the hospital less than a week after Hurricane Hugo and the switch."

Harley flipped through the file and pulled out a photograph that he handed over to Jade. She took it from him, studying the picture of the woman with the bright red curls and round face. She looked like she would have the cheery, chatty disposition that the mothers had mentioned from their time in the hospital. It was hard to believe that a week later, this woman would be dead.

"She jumped from the roof. My gut feeling is that it isn't a coincidence. I think the CEO said something about her having a drinking problem that may have driven the suicide, but I'm going to do some digging. It sounds more like the action of someone with a guilty conscience to me."

Harley's words triggered a memory in Jade's mind, but she couldn't put her finger on it immediately. "What did you say?"

"It just seems like the actions of a guilty conscience."

We've sat on our hands for three decades because of her stupid conscience...

"Wait." Jade put her hands up to silence Harley. "That's it. That's what they said in the van."

"Who?"

"My kidnappers. One of them was complaining about the other guy's sister having an attack of conscience that ruined their plans. Do you think that's what they meant?"

"It could be. Do you remember anything else?"

Jade stared at the photo and tried to remember the argument she'd listened to as she banged around in the back of her abductor's van. "I think one of them said she was dead, but she hadn't told them what they needed to know."

"Like which baby was which?"

She frowned. She wished she could remember more. She'd tried to memorize every moment, but between the stress and shock of the abduction, a lot of the details had become hazy in her mind over the last few weeks. "Could be. Did Nancy have a brother? That would definitely be a starting point. If not, it's a dead end."

Harley scanned the file and pointed at the emergency contact box. "She listed her next of kin as her brother. Gregory Crowley. Does that sound familiar?"

Jade shrugged. "I don't think they used names. But one was definitely the brother. I'm not sure about the other guy, though."

She watched as he turned to his notes and flipped through to what he'd written down after listening to the recorded discussion he'd had with the retired hospital CEO. "He mentioned a brother and a boyfriend when he talked about Nancy's suicide. How upset they both were. I'll see if I can get any more information about her death from the local authorities. If this is the right lead, they could've been upset for an entirely different reason."

Jade crossed her arms over her chest and shook her head. "Sounds like Nancy may have switched the babies and then took the secret with her to the grave."

"You're home awfully late, missy."

Morgan stopped in the grand foyer of her parents' mansion and turned toward the library. There, she saw her brother Sawyer sitting in an armchair reading one of the leather-bound volumes their father collected.

"You sound like Dad."

Sawyer flipped the book shut, setting it aside before getting up and walking out into the bright lights of the glittering chandelier that hung overhead in the entrance. His gaze narrowed at her for a moment. "You take that back," he quipped and then smiled.

"Where is Dad?" she asked.

"That's a good question. He asked me to come over tonight to discuss some work stuff, but he must've gotten caught up at the office. I haven't seen him yet. I can tell it's getting late because Lena keeps trying to feed me. She's finally given up, but every time she walks by, she clucks her tongue."

"You might as well give in and eat."

Sawyer sighed and looked down at the Patek Philippe watch he'd gotten for Christmas from their parents. "I will if you will."

"That's fair. I haven't had dinner yet."

That was true enough. They'd had a couple drinks, but Morgan had been careful not to let the evening with River evolve into more. Drinks could lead to dinner, which could lead to…breakfast. She couldn't let that happen. So she'd politely made her exit after her second chardonnay and headed back to the house. In truth, she was starving now.

The kitchen was dimly lit and immaculately clean when they went in. Lena was nowhere to be found, likely having retired to her quarters for the evening.

"She must've given up on all of us," Sawyer said.

"We can find something for ourselves." Morgan walked over to the giant Sub-Zero refrigerator and opened the double doors. There was every kind of fresh produce and dairy product imaginable. Dozens of neat containers lined the shelves with diced and prepared ingredients that Lena probably had ready for the next day's meals. She knew to steer clear of that.

Reaching inside, she grabbed a block of cheddar and a stick of butter. "Get the French bread off the counter and slice up a few pieces. We're making grilled cheese."

Sawyer looked dubious, but did as he was told.

"Since when do you cook?" he asked as he held up a skillet like it might bite him. "You keep the local Chinese restaurant in your contacts list."

"I can make grilled cheese. You went to college, didn't you?"

"We had meal plans," he pointed out. "I ate three squares in the campus cafeteria. Didn't you?"

"Well…yes. But the food courts weren't open 24/7. I can make grilled cheese." She pulled a very sharp looking knife from the block on the counter and eyed the thick chunk of cheddar. This wasn't the prewrapped individual slices she remembered from the grocery store. Slicing this poorly could cost her the tip of her thumb if she weren't careful. The bread also looked crusty and treacherous. She should've known that Lena wouldn't be caught dead with processed cheese or presliced white bread in her kitchen.

"We can do this," she insisted. "We are adults. We damn near run a company. There are people our age with children and homes that they manage on their own. Certainly, we're capable of making ourselves dinner. Right?"

Ten minutes later, with the butter and cheese back in the refrigerator where they belonged, Sawyer and Morgan settled in the upstairs family room with their old standby from their youth: a bag of tortilla chips, a jar of salsa and a container of cookies Lena had baked earlier. As kids, they had liked to sneak down into the kitchen late at night and find unhealthy contraband to take up and eat while they played video games. The kitchen was just as alien to them now as it was then.

The family room, however, was where they'd spent their youth. It was the center of the "kids' wing" with each of the children's bedrooms surrounding the large common area. It was one of the only places in the house that they could do whatever they wanted. When they were young, it was a playroom with their toys, and as they got older, it evolved to include a big-screen television, all their video game systems and a foosball table. It even had its own minibar with a microwave, sink, small fridge and stash of healthy snacks for growing children. Unfortunately, it hadn't been stocked with anything other than bottled water since Morgan had moved away to college.

Morgan settled onto the large sectional sofa and laid out their makeshift dinner on the coffee table while Sawyer got some cold water bottles for them. She kicked off her heels and curled her feet up on the couch. It felt amazing to finally take her shoes off after a long day. She really didn't like wearing them, but she was significantly shorter than the rest of the family and it was how she'd made up for that genetic shortcoming.

"So where were you this afternoon? I came by

your office to ask you something and your assistant said you'd already left for the day. Playing hooky?"

"Hardly," she said. "I was meeting with this summer's contractor to look at some land we're going to buy."

"And yet you smell like a sports bar. How does that work?"

Morgan rolled her eyes and opened the bag of chips. "Yes, well, we went for a drink afterward." She tried opening the jar of salsa and struggled.

"What's going on with that guy?" Sawyer asked. He took the jar from her and opened it easily. "River, right? That's a weird name."

Morgan frowned. "I don't know what you're talking about. Nothing is going on. And you're one to talk, when all of the kids in our family are named after Mark Twain characters."

"No changing the subject. I know a lot of personal crap has happened since the party, so I didn't bring it up earlier, but it's been long enough now. What's up between you two? When I introduced him to you, there was something going on there."

She knew there were a couple different ways she could go with this. Outright lie. Lie by omission. Tell the truth. Or tell enough truth to make it believable but still mostly lie. Of her three brothers, Sawyer was the most insightful one. Just like he had noticed something between Morgan and River, he would also be the most likely to know she wasn't being honest with him.

"We met back in college," she said. "I hadn't seen him in years and didn't know he was involved with this year's project, so it was a surprise." There. Just enough truth, but all the salacious details were missing.

"Did you guys date back then or something?" Sawyer was reading between the lines, as she'd feared. "I noticed he looked at you with more than a casual appreciation in his eyes."

"I looked good that night," Morgan said in a conceitedly confident tone. "But yes, we did date. Briefly. Nothing came of it. You know Dad wouldn't have allowed it."

Sawyer nodded. While he didn't have the same pressures put on him as Morgan did as the only daughter, he still pursued romance cautiously. All the young Steeles had social-climbing targets on their backs. Sawyer and Tom fought off most of their obvious pursuers, unlike Finn, who jumped into the Charleston dating pool feet first.

"And what about now?" He leaned forward to grab the container of cookies and peeled off the lid. "Snickerdoodles," he groaned, and inhaled the addictive scent of cinnamon and butter.

Morgan reached out to take one. "What do you mean?" she asked cautiously.

"Oh, come on. There's still something there. You guys went out for a drink. Do you think anything is going to come of it? I mean, you're a grown woman now. You don't have to worry about what Dad thinks of your relationships anymore."

Morgan wasn't entirely sure that was true, at least in her case, but it was an interesting thought. A lot had changed in her life since the day her father hauled her out of her honeymoon cabin. While she didn't entirely trust River's motivations—this could still all be about money for him, then and now—she could protect herself by knowing that going in.

"I don't know what it is, Sawyer. Probably nothing more than a little reminiscing. Or maybe he's just looking for his second shot at landing the Steele heiress."

"On a point of technicality, you aren't the Steele heiress anymore."

Morgan frowned at him. "Am I being disinherited without my knowledge?"

"No, of course not. You know our parents would never even think of such a thing. I meant that with everything that has come to light lately, perhaps you should shake off the mantle of heiress and do what you want with your life for a change. You hold back. You always have. And I get it. Dad watches you closer than any of us. But you're about to turn thirty. You need to stop worrying about what other people think—especially Dad—and live your life."

Morgan and Sawyer rarely had time to sit and have real discussions without the rest of the family around. Without Finn to make a joke or Tom changing the subject when things got heavy or uncomfortable, there was nothing for her to do but seriously think about what her brother had said.

And he was right. She didn't have to be the perfect Steele daughter any longer. Maybe she could try living her life for a while as Morgan Nolan and see how that worked out.

There was a lot of history between Morgan and River. More than anyone, even River, knew about. A lot of reasons why opening up this Pandora's box was a bad idea. And yet, all the original reasons why she couldn't have River were off the table now. And despite how much she didn't want to be attracted to him, she couldn't help herself. There was something there—something Morgan couldn't fight—that drew her to him. And the more time she spent with him, the worse it got. He was a good guy, contrary to the villain her father had painted him to be. Maybe she'd been wrong this whole time.

"I'm not saying you run off and marry the guy," Sawyer continued, "but what can it hurt to indulge a little? You're both adults. You're attracted to one another. Take the proper precautions and do what you want to do. It's time to live your own life, Morgan."

She had never expected to have this kind of re-alization tonight, especially with her brother's help, but he was right. Regardless of who her parents were or how she'd been raised, she was an adult now. This was Morgan's life and she was going to live it.

Five

River was pleased with himself. He tried not to be too arrogant, but there were two things he knew better than anything else—construction and Morgan. Since finding a place for her to live combined both those skill sets, he was pretty confident that she would love what he showed her.

He was right.

That's why he'd suggested that instead of meeting in the office today, they should come here to his latest property instead. He had called that morning to let her know their offer had been accepted on the downtown land purchase. Everything was being finalized. He just needed her to sign a few things before they broke ground and got started building the houses.

She'd agreed to meet him later that afternoon. Now they were in a town house on the peninsula where he'd recently completed the renovations. Originally part of an 1840s warehouse, it had been converted into a row of town houses a hundred years later. This project had been more art than skill, trying to balance historic details like the original brick facade with the sleek quartz and modern bath and kitchen fixtures that buyers wanted.

At the moment, he was sitting in the bench seat of the bay window, watching Morgan wander through the place. He wanted to give her time to explore on her own and she was taking advantage of it. Her wide eyes seemed to take in every detail as her fingertips grazed over different surfaces. She hadn't even spoken to him since she'd signed the paperwork on the kitchen island. She gasped as she spied the original heart pine floors in the living room, and he knew he had her. The place had only been staged a few days ago, but he got the feeling he hadn't needed to bother with the expense.

"This is amazing work," she said at last. There was a flush to Morgan's cheeks as she turned to him. He recognized that expression. It was love. At one time, she'd looked at him that way. Now he'd have to settle for her loving his handiwork. "It's stunning, really."

River got up and walked over to where she was standing and admiring the fireplace with the original glazed tile surround. "I'm glad you like it."

"The location is amazing, too. It's so close to Broad Street and Waterfront Park. It doesn't get much better than that in Charleston."

"That's what I thought when I found the place up for sale. It needed a lot of work—I think they hadn't renovated since the '80s—but I thought it was worth it. You haven't even seen the upstairs yet. You'll adore the master bath, I'm pretty sure."

Morgan's eyes lit up. She turned toward the staircase and this time he followed her upstairs. She explored the three bedrooms and the luxurious Carrara marble bath, then turned to look at him with a suspicious narrowed gaze. "You set me up, didn't you?"

"What do you mean?"

She crossed her arms over her chest, drawing his attention to the press of her firm breasts against her shirt. "You said it would be easier to meet here, but you really just wanted me to see the place. We could've met anywhere, but you knew I'd love it."

River could only shrug as he shifted his gaze back to her eyes. "How could you not love it? It's an amazing town house. Yes, I set you up," he admitted with a grin. "But I only wanted you to see it before I put it

on the market in case you had to have it. I expect it
to sell pretty quickly when I do, so I didn't want you
to miss your chance. There's no pressure."

She sighed and turned back to admire the original crown molding in the master bedroom. He followed her gaze as it fell onto the king-size bed and
plush headboard on the center of the far wall. Normally, his stager would've used a queen bed, but the
room was big enough to accommodate a larger one.

"I already have a place. In DC. I don't need a
house here, River."

"I thought it was a rental."

"Does that make a difference? It's still a home in
a town I love."

"Then don't buy it," he said dismissively. "I only
wanted you to know you have options. There's no
reason for you to spend every summer living with
your parents. You're a grown woman—almost
thirty—with the financial means to do whatever
you want. As much as you come back to town, I'd
think you'd want your own space here in Charleston. Even just as an investment property. The market here is pretty hot."

"Thanks for the reminder of how old I am," she
said with a cutting, sarcastic tone. "What you don't
quite understand is how large my parents' home really is. With all the boys in their own places, I basi-

cally have an upstairs wing of the mansion to myself. It's not like I'm tripping over my parents."

River took a step closer to her, closing the gap between them. He stretched one arm out and braced it on the doorway as he leaned in. He didn't crowd her personal space, but he was close enough to feel her warm breath as she exhaled and smell the scent of her perfume. "So you can do whatever you like, right? How about entertain a gentleman?"

Her gaze nervously met his and her tongue shot out to wet her bottom lip. She didn't have to answer that out loud. They both knew her father didn't care if she was fifteen, thirty or fifty, there would be none of that under his roof. He was as overprotective as he ever was.

"That hasn't been an issue," she said. "I come to Charleston to work, nothing more. I'm too busy to worry much about a personal life these days."

There was something about the way she looked at him when she spoke. Something that made him want to move closer, even as she insisted she didn't have time for a physical relationship. "It sounds to me like all you do is work. All work and no play makes Morgan a dull girl."

Morgan's green-gold eyes focused on his lips as he spoke. The memories of their brief, innocent kiss at the empty plot of land flooded his mind as he looked at her. It hadn't been a great, passionate connection in reality, and yet it had felt that way. Kissing Morgan was the same as it had always been—like being struck by lightning. His whole body lit up at her touch, every nerve alive with wanting her.

In that instant, it was as though the last decade and the drama that drove them apart had never happened. To force himself to move on, he'd told himself so many things. That she hadn't loved him. That she was just a spoiled rich girl using him to get back at Daddy. That the connection they'd shared was nothing special.

But when she'd touched him again, he knew it had all been lies. She might've regretted moving too fast and bent to her father's will, but he hadn't imagined the magnetic draw they shared. It was just as strong as it had ever been.

"Trust me," he said. "I'm an expert on working too much." River dropped his arm to his side and moved closer. He looked down at her, only inches away, but she didn't move. "You can ignore your needs…push them aside…but they don't go away. They build up inside of you. A burning, churning feeling in your belly. Eventually, you have to let off the pressure or you'll do something stupid."

Morgan's gaze didn't move from his own. Instead, she put a hand on his chest and her lips parted softly in invitation. "Something stupid like this?" she asked with an arched brow.

Her touch was searing through the cotton of his dress shirt. The heat made his brain start to short circuit, making the idea of having her be all he could think about. "That's...*debatable*. If you'd asked me a week ago, I'd have said it was a bad idea. A terrible idea. But if you're going to keep touching me like that, I will argue this is the perfect way to let off steam. I'd be happy to, uh, help you in that department."

He was rambling nervously, but he couldn't stop the flow of words. Not when she was this close and looking at him the way she was.

Morgan ran her palm over his chest, sliding it up the side of his neck to cradle the back of his skull. He closed his eyes and leaned into her touch. "That's very kind of you."

"Morgan..." His breath caught in his throat as he said her name. If she was just flirting, she was playing a dangerous game. He wanted her. If she didn't want him, she needed to step away.

She didn't. She pulled his head down until their lips met. It was an explosive kiss, the contact igniting the fire inside of River that he'd fought to keep down. Any reservations he might have had about tasting Morgan again fizzled away as she bit his bottom lip and he groaned aloud.

She'd gotten feistier than he remembered her to be. He liked that. A lot. River wasn't sure who moved how, but one moment, they were standing and the next, he was pressing her body into the mattress previously beside them. There wasn't a break, not a hesitation, but an evolution of their kiss. It deepened, it intensified and with it, River felt the desperation start to bubble up inside of him.

He'd been telling the truth when he told Morgan he knew what it was like to work too much and deny himself. He was an expert at that. But he couldn't deny himself any longer. Not when it came to Morgan.

His hands roamed over her body, reacquainting themselves with the terrain that had changed some since he'd last touched it. Her breasts were fuller as he cupped one through her thin cotton T-shirt. He could feel the tight bud of her nipple pressing through the fabric of her bra as though it were reaching out for his touch. That much, at least, hadn't changed. She had always responded to him like that.

Then he let his hand glide down her stomach. He wanted to keep exploring. To seek out the heat hidden beneath her slacks…but she tensed up beneath him. Suddenly, she was stiff as a board beneath his touch, bringing his worst fear to life. Her mouth jerked away from his, even as her hand caught his wrist and pulled him away from her belly.

"River, stop," she said in a harsh whisper. The

eyes that had been looking at him with barely masked desire were now wide and startled.

River immediately pulled back. "What's wrong?"

Her gaze met his for only a second before she rolled away from him and got off the bed. He thought he saw a shimmer of tears in her eyes as she turned her back to him. "Nothing," she said. "I have to go." She rushed to the door and disappeared to the thumping sound of her feet pounding down the stairs. He heard the front door slam and knew she was gone.

What the hell?

He pushed himself to the foot of the bed, tugging his own shirt down and running his hands over his beard in exasperation. His groin was throbbing with interrupted desire as he turned to look at the rumpled comforter they'd lain on a moment before. He didn't understand what had gone wrong.

And he got the feeling Morgan didn't have any intention of telling him.

"What the hell do I think I'm doing?"

Morgan shook her head as she pulled away from the town house and left it, and River, behind. She'd come to sign paperwork. Just some paperwork. And yet, somehow, she'd ended up on her back and on the verge of giving everything away she'd tried so hard to keep secret.

She navigated through the narrow busy streets

of downtown Charleston with an angry grip on the wheel, heading for the bridge that would take her over the water toward her parents' home in Mount Pleasant. Her frustration lessened the farther she got from River, but the dull ache of need remained.

Making peace with him was a bad idea. Fighting wasn't ideal, but it made it easier to keep her distance. Without that wall of resentment between them, she was just putty in his hands. She had thought that was okay. Her chat with Sawyer had convinced her she was a grown woman and could do what she liked. And that had seemed like a good idea. Until River's hand ran across her stomach and the reality of her situation set in.

She and River may have called a truce on how their marriage ended, but she knew that would be short-lived if he knew everything. There were some secrets that needed to be kept. Especially if the Steele housing project was going to be completed smoothly this year. River couldn't know the truth because it was so inflammatory, so damaging that it would hurt more than the lie.

That's what she'd told herself ten years ago as she sat on her dorm room mattress, staring at a positive pregnancy test. She was pregnant with River's child.

Up until that point, she had lived firmly in denial. There was no way she was pregnant because her father had wiped the past from the record books. She never married River, according to the state of Tennessee. They never had a honeymoon. So she couldn't possibly be pregnant. There was no way she was carrying the baby of the guy who had hit her dad up for cash and disappeared from her life. Fate wouldn't be that cruel. And as such, she ignored the signs, popping antacids and struggling to focus in her classes that fall.

Her dropping GPA wasn't the only sign of trouble. Once Christmas break came around, there was no more denying the truth. Not to herself and certainly not to her parents. When her mother arrived to pick her up for the holiday, her gaze had immediately dropped to the rounding belly that Morgan was trying to hide beneath a USC sweatshirt.

From there, it was a whirlwind that Morgan almost didn't remember. Her parents went into instant damage-control mode, and she was just along for the ride. No one was to know the truth, they decided. Not even her brothers. For her own protection and that of her reputation, of course. Her parents had successfully kept her short marriage a secret from everyone, and they were confident they could keep the baby a hush-hush topic, too.

They bought her older brothers a luxurious ski trip in Aspen for Christmas, sending them off to Colorado instead of having them celebrate at home that year. As far as anyone knew, Morgan had the flu and couldn't attend any events with them. Her only outings were to the doctor for her checkups.

She hadn't bothered to argue with them about it. Her spirit had been crushed when she lost what she thought she'd had with River, and nothing else mattered. Part of her wanted to keep their baby so she'd always have a piece of him with her, but she worried the child would only be a painful reminder of his ultimate betrayal.

Morgan hadn't known what to do, but it was all a mess of her own making, so she decided that perhaps she'd be better served letting her parents choose the best course. She hadn't been sure if they were going to send her off to Switzerland or something to have the child in secret and give it up for adoption, let her keep it, or raise it as their own, and she never did find out. Their plans ended up not mattering in the end.

At twenty-five weeks, just a few days after Christmas, something went wrong. She just didn't feel right and went in to see her obstetrician. Morgan's blood pressure was through the roof. She sat in a hospital room for a week, spending New Year's Eve under the doctors' careful watch while they tried to get it down. They hadn't wanted to deliver the baby that early. It was risky. Too risky, even with the latest technology. But it was a dangerous situation for Morgan, too. Soon it became clear they didn't have a choice or they would lose them both.

Dawn Mackenzie Steele had been born via emergency C-section and weighed a little over a pound. Morgan never got to hold her, but if she had, the tiny infant could've fit in the palm of her hand. She hadn't known what she wanted to do until she saw her daughter covered in tubes and wires in an incubator. Then, more than anything, she wanted her baby. She didn't care what her parents wanted or thought. She wasn't concerned about scandal or what people would say. She just wanted Dawn to be okay. But that wouldn't happen. The neonatal intensive care staff did everything they could, but Dawn's little lungs just weren't ready for the outside world.

Morgan didn't realize she was crying at the wheel until the road started to blur around her. She pulled her car over into a shopping center and turned off the engine. She hugged her stomach like she had after Dawn was gone and rested her head against the steering wheel.

The tears flowed freely then. It had been a long time since she'd cried for Dawn. Years, maybe, as she'd tried to put her past in the past and focus on her future. That's what her father had told her to do. He'd held her as she cried. She was his baby girl after all, and he hated that she was hurting. But he came from an upbringing that felt the best way to cope was to forget and move forward.

It was sad… It was unfortunate, he'd said, but

perhaps this was her second chance at having the kind of life he'd always dreamed of for her. She was so young with so much ahead of her. He was certain she would have her babies some day in the future, with a good man who adored her and cared for her the way she deserved.

Trevor Steele's words fell on deaf ears, although he never knew it. Then, and even now, there was a part of Morgan that never wanted to marry and have children. She'd tried it once and failed. She wasn't sure her heart could take the pain of failing at all of it again. So she'd focused on finishing school, concentrated on her work, made sure she was the good daughter they wanted.

And she got the hell out of South Carolina.

A quiet tap at the car window startled Morgan out of her tears. She looked out to see a little old man watching her with concern as he clutched a sack of groceries from the store she'd stopped at.

She rolled down the window, self-consciously wiping the mascara-stained tears from her cheeks. "Yes?"

"Are you okay, dear? Is there something I can do?"

Morgan put on her best practiced smile and shook her head. "No, I'm fine. I just need a minute. You're sweet to check on me, though. Thank you."

The man nodded and smiled back, but she could

tell he didn't believe her. "Have a good day," he said instead, and continued on to his car.

Morgan rolled up the window and pulled her visor mirror down to fix her face. Her skin was red and blotchy from the tears and her eye makeup was everywhere. She pulled a tissue from her purse to do what she could, blew her nose and got back on the road before anyone else came to check on her.

When she pulled in at her parents' house, she didn't go inside immediately. Instead, she went around the back of the house toward the gardens. There, beyond the entertaining spaces, right at the edge of some trees, there was a stone bench. Beside it, a marble plaque that was nearly invisible if you weren't looking for it in the grass.

What seemed like a nice place to sit and enjoy the gardens was actually the world's tiniest graveyard. Her family had an ostentatious mausoleum at Magnolia Cemetery where generations of Steeles were laid to rest, but after she lost Dawn, her father had had a small private graveyard designated on their property. He told her that he wanted her to be able to visit whenever she wanted to. It didn't hurt that no one would see it back there, either.

She approached the site more slowly as she got closer. Despite how close it was, it had been a long time since she'd come back here. In part, because when Morgan had buried her daughter, she'd buried that part of her life with her. Or at least she'd tried to. River's sudden reappearance in her life had changed everything.

Morgan lowered herself down onto the bench and looked at the marble slab that marked her baby's grave. It said simply *Dawn Steele,* with a single date. Her life had been so short there was only one date to put there.

She reached down and ran her fingertips across the cold stone. The site was immaculately kept. The family gardener, Paul, was probably paid hand-somely to maintain it in the strictest confidence. He was one of only a handful of people who knew about Dawn. Aside from her parents, only Lena had been around to know the truth. She'd brought her prena-tal vitamins and ice cream each night before Dawn was born, then her collection of pills with her favorite sparkling water and a few fresh cookies each night after she was born.

Since then, perhaps everyone except Paul had for-gotten about this tiny grave and the child it was for. Suddenly, the thought of Dawn made her incred-ibly sad.

Being around River again had done more than stir up old feelings of desire and regret. It had reminded her that there was more at stake here than just an-other successful charity project.

That was what had caused the panic as she lay

with River in the town house. The moment his hand brushed over her stomach, the reality of her situation came rushing in. She couldn't let River touch her. See her. Not there, like that. He would see the scar in the bright afternoon daylight. He would notice the firm belly he remembered was soft and covered in faded stretch marks. He would want to know the truth and she couldn't bear to tell him what had happened. He would hate her. Hate her and her family for hiding the truth from him.

Back then, when she could still feel her daughter moving inside of her, she'd wondered if she needed to reach out to River. Whether he had been using her for money or not, this was his child. He may not have been the man she thought he was, but he deserved to know the truth. Then, before she could tell him he had a daughter, she was gone. What good would telling him do now? It would only cause him unnecessary pain. And even though she wouldn't admit it to herself, she'd still loved River. She couldn't intentionally hurt him.

So she kept quiet. Looked to the future. And tried to forget.

"I'm so sorry," she said to her daughter's tombstone as her eyes welled up with tears again. "You deserved better than what you went through. You deserved a life. Love. We both did. And I screwed it all up for us."

Six

Not a word. Not a single word, work-related or otherwise, in two weeks! The land was purchased and leveled, the plumbing was run and the slabs were poured and in the process of curing for all three houses. Framing was going up tomorrow and the roofs after that. And yet, Morgan hadn't spoken to him since she'd run from the town house that afternoon.

River stood in the lobby of Steele Tools, trying to decide if he should go upstairs and confront Morgan. He did need to talk to her about some business-related topics, but he knew those could've been handled via email. The truth was that he was here on a personal mission.

She walked out on him. In the middle of...well, the worst possible time to walk out. There was no explanation, no nothing. She'd run from his life once without another word. He wasn't about to let that happen a second time. If she didn't want him, if she had regrets about back then and now, she was going to tell him to his face without Daddy running interference.

He straightened his tie and was about to head toward the elevator when he heard an odd sound. It was something akin to a sputter and a gasp mixed together. He expected it to be Morgan, but then he turned to his left and found he was suddenly face-to-face with her father—Trevor Steele.

He expected the man to yell. Trevor had certainly done his share of that when he'd stolen River's wife from his bed all those years ago, but now, there was only an eerie silence as the man stared him down.

River was older now. Less intimated by a man like Trevor than he was back then. He wasn't a kid anymore, playing at being a man. Instead, he grinned and stuck out his hand to greet him. "Mr. Steele! Good to see you again, sir."

The man narrowed his gaze but didn't return the smile. "What are you doing here, River?" he asked in a voice so low River almost couldn't hear it.

That's when he remembered what Morgan had said about her parents. They hated scandal. Trevor would probably love to beat River with his briefcase, but he wouldn't because that would cause a scene. "You don't know, sir? My company is working with yours to build houses for the less fortunate."

River watched as the muscles in Trevor's neck and jaw tightened until he thought they might pop through his skin. "Is this my daughter's doing?" he asked coolly.

"Not at all. I believe my company was chosen through a downselect process overseen by one of your sons." River smiled as brightly as he could manage at the scowling man. Trevor Steele's firm policy of secrecy had bitten him in this case. "I'm not surprised they chose me. I took your advice and made the most of the bribe you gave me. I'm quite successful these days."

"A bribe?!" Trevor sputtered as he glanced around the lobby to see if anyone was nearby. "You keep your voice down when you throw around accusations like that. It was no such thing."

He crossed his arms over his chest and eyeballed the older man thoughtfully. "What would you call paying me to leave and never speak to your daughter again, sir?"

"I would call it softening the blow."

River laughed at the man's internal justification.

You can't have my daughter, but here's a hundred grand for your troubles, son. "Is that what you tell yourself so you can sleep at night?"

"I sleep very well, or I did when I thought you were out of my daughter's life for good."

"As far as your precious daughter is concerned, I am out of her life. No worries there," River added with a bitterness he couldn't hide. He still wasn't sure what had sent her running and kept her silent for the last two weeks, but he was going to get to the bottom of it. That is, if security didn't toss him out of the building before he got the chance.

"Good. Keep it that way." Trevor started to turn his back and walk away.

"Of course, she doesn't know the truth," River called after him.

Trevor froze and turned back to River. "What truth?"

"I'm not sure, but she seems really upset with me about that money. Almost like it was my idea."

Trevor stiffened at his words. He had lied to his daughter and now River was calling him out on it.

"At first," River continued, "I thought maybe she was just angry because I took the money you offered. Honestly, I quarreled with myself about accepting it, but when it came down to it, I had nothing else left. Then I wondered if maybe she thought she was worth more than a hundred grand to me. But talking to you now, I think I've realized the real issue. She thinks I *made* you pay me to go away. Like I was just after her money the whole time and hit you up for cash to go away quietly."

Trevor crossed his arms over his chest. "You did take the money and go away quietly, River. That's a natural conclusion for her to make under the circumstances."

River shook his head. "No. No, I think she believes it because that's what you told her. You lied and told her I demanded money to agree to the annulment. I'm sure it made it easier to get her away from me if she thought I was just some poor scum after whatever cash I could get. I couldn't possibly have really loved her, right?"

Trevor looked down dispassionately at his watch and shrugged. "If that's what you want to believe—if that makes losing her more palatable for you—then fine."

"I should tell her the truth. She deserves to know you lied to her to break us up."

"I have an important meeting to get to. I don't have time to argue with you, River. But know this," Trevor said, leaning in close to him. "You do not want to start unearthing the past. Morgan has spent years trying to get over everything that happened. It has been a long time now and it seems like both of you have done well on your own. I can only hope that you will be smart about this and let sleeping dogs lie. Nothing but pain will come from stirring things up. Good day, Mr. Atkinson."

Trevor marched across the marble lobby floors, leaving River alone, stewing in his aggravation.

There was probably some wisdom in the older man's words. Things might be better left alone. But they also might be better if everyone knew the truth. That all depended on Morgan.

Taking a deep breath, he headed toward the elevator and pressed the button to head up to her office.

Greg Crowley blew through the back door of his father's home with a scowl of irritation on his face. He'd spent another day downtown trying to get some day-labor work for cash under the table and had come home with twenty bucks in his pocket. Not exactly where he pictured he would be after his ten-million-dollar payday only a month or so ago.

He chucked his ratty backpack onto the kitchen chair and went into the living room. His elderly father was sitting in his recliner, watching television. That was basically all the man had done for the last twenty years since Greg and Nancy's mother passed away. Watch TV and collect his pension.

He turned to the television in time to see they were talking about the Steele kidnapping case again. That's all they seemed to talk about on the local news these days. Or maybe it just seemed that way because of his conscience. Either way it made him nervous. "Turn that shit off, Dad. No one wants to hear about some rich girl's problems."

"Meh!" his father groaned and didn't budge his remote thumb an inch.

Rolling his eyes, Greg returned to the kitchen for a can of beer and carried it with him back into his bedroom. It was the same bedroom he'd grown up in. With the same damn twin mattress that had been lumpy and awful then, much less now. Living with his father again hadn't been ideal, but now this was his only haven. The only place in the world he felt safe.

No thanks to Buster.

Maybe Greg was naïve. He'd known Buster for over thirty years. That seemed like the kind of friendship that could be considered trustworthy, even if they shared a common bond of being criminals. He was wrong. After they made off with Jade Nolan's ransom money, Buster insisted they lay low for a bit. By the time Greg looked up from his hiding place a week later, he realized Buster was long gone and so was the money. Every damn cent.

He hadn't even wanted to go along with this whole plot. Not back then, and not now, either. It was Nancy and Buster who had been gung ho about it. His sister had gotten the idea after the Steeles were admitted to St. Francis, then discharged for false contractions. Nancy knew they would be back to deliver their child soon enough. That gave them just enough time to formulate their plan. Kidnapping the Steele baby outright wouldn't fly. Someone had already abducted their eldest a few years before and it was in all the papers. They needed a different angle and they found it.

It seemed simple enough. Swap the babies. Send the Steele infant home with an unsuspecting couple. Their home wouldn't have security, alarms, cameras or nannies watching the child 24/7 like they had at the Steele mansion. They would then kidnap the Steele infant from the regular couple, then call the Steeles, inform them of the switch and demand the ransom money.

It was a simple enough payday. No one got hurt. The baby would be returned, the parents would get their correct children back and they could all retire with pockets full of Steele family cash.

Hurricane Hugo hadn't been a part of the plan, but it made things easier. Nancy had no trouble swapping the infants' ID bands in the chaos. She had access to the names and address of the couple that would take the Steele daughter home with them. Everything was going according to plan. Until it wasn't.

Greg never expected everything to go so spectacularly wrong. He couldn't have even imagined it because he hadn't realized how bad his sister's drinking had become. Or how serious her depression had gotten. She hid it well behind a cheery exterior. But the next thing he knew, his sister was dead and the Steele baby's location was lost with her.

When Nancy went into the ground, he thought—or hoped at least—that that would be the end of it. For years, he watched his parents struggle with losing Nancy. The stress of it eventually killed their mother. Greg tried to move on with his life and put his criminal phase behind him. And he'd succeeded. He'd had a steady job, a nice enough apartment and a lady friend he went to dinner with from time to time.

Then Buster showed up one day pointing to an article in the newspaper about some big hospital mix-up thirty years ago. Now they had the piece of the puzzle they were missing—Jade Nolan was the Steele heiress. Buster was convinced this was their chance to get the payday they were owed at last. Greg wasn't as enthused. He would've rather the woman just keep her mouth shut and let it go. He'd sent threatening letters and even ransacked her house to scare her off the case.

But as always, Buster got his way. Greg quit his job to help Buster plan. He wouldn't need the work once he was rich, right? Then they kidnapped the Steele woman and for once in his life, he thought things were finally looking up.

As Greg looked around his childhood bedroom,

he realized that his whole life had been a waste. Whatever he'd wanted to be, whatever he'd hoped to become had been taken from him. Taken by Nancy. Taken by Buster. Even taken by those mixed-up babies at the hospital. He couldn't blame any of them for what had happened. At least not Nancy and Buster. It was too late for that with his sister in the ground and Buster vanished.

But it wasn't too late to blame the Steele family. They dangled their wealth and privilege around town, just daring people to take a chance at getting a cut for themselves, then crushing anyone who tried.

For a while, Greg thought he could start over again. Maybe he could get the job back and give that lady friend a call. But the more he thought about it, the more he realized that time was long gone. He was fifty-six, unemployed, broke and sleeping on a lumpy twin bed in his father's home. He had nothing to offer and nothing left to lose.

And that made him dangerous.

Morgan looked up from her computer to find River standing in her doorway. She glanced at her phone, wondering what had happened to her receptionist and gatekeeper, then remembered she had left early today for an appointment.

Of all the days...

"That's not excitement to see me," River said as

he stepped into her office and shut the door behind him. "It's almost like you've been hiding from me for two weeks and finally got caught."

"I haven't been hiding. I've been…busy." That was a terrible answer, but the best Morgan could come up with on the spot. She sighed and shut her laptop down, then she stood up and came out from behind her desk. She was hoping to intercept River before he sat in her guest chair and got comfortable, but he just sauntered over to the conference table and leaned against it instead. He crossed his arms over his chest and narrowed his gaze at her.

"Busy? Busy doing everything to avoid talking about what happened is more like it."

Morgan's tight lips twisted as she sought out the right words to respond. She had decided that honesty was not the best policy in this case, especially after all this time, but she hadn't come up with a better story, either. "I'm sorry about that," she said. "It was rude."

"Rude?" he chuckled. "Rude is saying you think I'm ugly. Or that dating me was the dumbest thing you ever did. Making out with me and then abandoning me with a serious case of blue balls is something else entirely."

She shook her head. "Were you always this crass and I just didn't notice it?"

"No. But I also wasn't this angry back then, either.

I hadn't met your father yet, of course, so my young idealism was still intact. But I just ran into him in the lobby. Seems you were right and he didn't realize I was working with you on the housing project. He was really excited to see me," he added with an upbeat tone despite the sarcastic bite of his words.

Morgan had been hoping her father would remain out of the loop concerning River, but unfortunately that hadn't worked out. She was certain she'd be hearing about his concerns posthaste. "No, I hadn't mentioned it. It didn't seem like a good idea, especially coming from me. Contracts were already signed at that point. He isn't involved with the project, so I was hoping it wouldn't matter. I couldn't very well explain to my brothers that there was a problem without telling them more than they needed to know."

"Your family and their secrets. It's not healthy the way you all keep them."

Morgan shrugged and slumped against the table beside him. It wasn't the best idea to stand this close to him, but it was better than looking him in the eye. When he looked at her that way, she was tempted to tell him everything she knew, and that was dangerous. "I'm sure we don't have any more secrets than any other family. Ours just tend to be on a larger scale. More dramatic than most. I guess it just comes with the territory."

"You mean with the money."

She shrugged. "As they say, more money, more problems. And I guess more secrets."

River sighed, standing silently beside her for a full minute before he spoke again. "What happened at the town house?" he asked quietly.

There were so many things she could say. Should say. And yet, she couldn't voice any of it out loud. Maybe later. Once the houses were built and their project together was at an end, maybe then she could tell him about Dawn. Then, when he hated her, they could go their separate ways.

The side of his hand brushed against her fingers and stole any concerns from her lips. It sent a thrill through her no matter how hard she tried to tamp it down. Eventually, Morgan would have to face that she and River had something that just couldn't be ignored.

"I got scared," she said at last. That, at least, was true enough.

"Of me?"

That forced her to turn and look him in the eyes. They were wary as they watched her. She'd hurt him on some level when she ran off the other day. She hadn't meant to, but she had. Perhaps it was too much like the last time when she'd left, only this time had been her choice, not her father's. "Of course not," she said emphatically. "I was scared of this. Us. This thing between us, whatever it is. I thought that after all this time, it might have lessened, but it hasn't. So I ran."

Her gaze dropped down to the knot of his silk tie and focused there instead of the face that was studying every one of her vulnerabilities. Then she felt the warm press of his hand against her cheek. He guided her back up to look at him. "You're not the only one that feels that way," he said.

Before she could really consider what that meant, his lips were on hers. She leaned into him, seeking out the comfort and protection he offered as he wrapped his arms around her. As a young woman, she'd always felt safe in River's arms. When she lost Dawn and everything seemed to be crumbling around her, she wanted his embrace more than anything else, and it was the one thing she couldn't have. But she could have it now. At least for a while.

"River?" She pulled away and whispered his name into the space between them.

An expression of physical pain flickered across his face for a moment. "You aren't about to run off again, are you? I'm not sure I can take that a second time."

"No. You're in *my* office, so I'm not going anywhere. I just wanted to talk about something before this went too much further."

"What?" His fingertips pressed into the curve of

her waist, massaging her hip as she spoke and making it hard for her to focus on her words.

"It's just that…well…I don't want anyone to find out about this. Whatever this is going on between us. If someone does, it will get ruined, I'm certain of it. I'd rather walk away now than have something with you spoiled again. Can we please keep it—whatever we decide we want it to be—just between us?"

He sighed and leaned back from her. His disappointment was palpable. "Great. Another Steele secret."

"It's not about keeping it a secret," she argued. "It's about not letting outside influences taint this. I want you. You want me. It's a simple thing. Neither of us is looking for anything more than a little comfort and release. Maybe some closure. But I don't want it to impact our professional work. Keeping this between us is the best way to make sure that doesn't happen. No drama, no scandal…nothing for Daddy to freak out over. Just a little fun between the two of us while it lasts."

"And after the key ceremony?"

Morgan brushed a strand of hair from his eyes. That event would mark the end of the project, as they handed over the keys to the new residents of the homes they'd built. It would be a bittersweet event for Morgan in more ways than one. "After the key ceremony, I think the best thing is for me to go back to DC and for you to go off and capitalize on the good work you've done here. That's the point of all this, right?"

"Right," he repeated, but she got the sense he wasn't content with this arrangement.

Did he want more? An actual relationship? Didn't he see how impossible that would be? It would be an uphill battle for them every step of the way until something drove them apart again. There was no sense in even entertaining something like that.

"You want me, don't you?" she asked.

His hands cupped her rear and pulled her tight against his erection. "You know I do."

"Then what's the matter? I thought you'd be happy. A no-strings affair with someone you have amazing chemistry with? That seems like a pretty sweet arrangement, especially considering both of us work too hard for anything more complicated."

"It's not that. The arrangement is fine. I guess I just want to know what's changed," he said.

Morgan pulled away and looked up at him. "What do you mean?"

"I mean, the last time we were together, you literally ran from the room. You said you were scared of what we had between us, and now you're practically crawling into my lap. What's different about this time? Is it the secrecy that makes you feel more secure? Are you ashamed of people knowing we're together, even casually?"

"Of course not. It has nothing to do with that." She reached up and stroked his cheek, feeling the coarse hairs of his beard tickle against her palm. It was an obvious reminder that he wasn't the boy she'd loved anymore. He was a man. A man that she wanted very badly, despite how she argued with herself. Over the last two weeks, she'd wrestled with how to move forward with River and get what she wanted without exposing the past she needed to keep hidden. For now, the best she could do was to try and keep parts of herself from being exposed so he wouldn't ask questions. Whether that entailed lingerie, dim lighting or her current strategy—staying partially clothed—it didn't matter. She was confident in her plan. If he was willing to go along with it.

"In the end, does it really matter why I changed my mind, as long as I have?" She looked at him with her mostly sultry gaze, hoping that it would make the answer moot.

"It shouldn't," River agreed. "I know I should just shut my mouth, thank the stars for the situation I'm currently in and take full advantage, but I guess I'm an ass and I overthink everything."

Morgan cradled his face in her hands and looked him in the eyes. "What's important is that I want you,

River. Every time I argue with myself about it, every time I deny what I need, it only makes me want you even more. What's different is that I know I can't run from it anymore. So as far as I'm concerned, there's only one thing left for us to do."

"What's that?" he asked.

"Lock my office door."

Seven

Morgan leaned back on the conference table with a mischievous smile, watching as River quickly rushed over to her door and flipped the lock. This was the moment they'd both been waiting for. She'd tried denying herself and running from her feelings, but it was clear that River wasn't going to let her avoid it any longer. The only thing to do was give in to what they both wanted, and she knew she could do it in a way that kept any questions at bay.

Her office was private and separated from the other Steele executives on the top floor. Her calendar was clear for the rest of the afternoon and her assistant was gone for the day. The only windows overlooked downtown, with no way for anyone to see what was about to happen in her corner office. It was the perfect place to indulge at last.

When he returned, he stopped just short of her and let his gaze dip down to study her body. She was still leaning against the conference table and she had no intention of moving. It was solid oak and just what they needed. For this first time at least, she wanted to take the edge off, not curl up together in bed and have pillow talk.

She hadn't planned for any of this to happen today, but her slinky pencil skirt and silk blouse would be perfect to unbutton and slide out of the way, and help hide any areas she didn't want River to see. His gaze moved over her thoughtfully, likely thinking the same thing as he planned his move.

River seemed either hesitant to reach for her or he wasn't in a rush. Morgan could understand that she'd jerked him around enough that he'd be waiting for her to change her mind. But not now. Not again. She needed to make sure he understood that. She reached out and wrapped her arms around his neck, pulling him closer. She looked up at him with a sly smirk curling her burgundy-painted lips.

"I want you, River. Right now. Right here."

That was enough to dash away his last concerns.

Now River snapped into action. Leaning past her with a quick slide of his arm, he moved a stack of papers and an arrangement of silk flowers on the table out of their way. Then he encircled her waist with his hands and lifted her up to sit at the edge of the smooth wood as though she weighed ten pounds. She closed her eyes and drank in the sensation as his palms slid up the silky length of her legs, pushing at the hem of her skirt. The fabric moved out of the way, allowing her to spread her thighs so River could find a home between them.

"Is this what you had in mind?" he asked, gripping her rear end and tugging her tight against the throbbing erection pressing against his trousers.

Morgan groaned softly, and then wrapped her legs around his waist. "Even better."

She leaned in to kiss River and the moment they touched, it was as though the floodgates had been opened. They'd been holding back for so long. This time there would be no interruption, no second thoughts. All the emotion and need that had built up over the last few weeks—and even the last ten years—came rushing forward at once. Their hands moved in a frenzy over each other's bodies, fighting with buttons and fasteners, tugging aside cotton and silk until they finally made contact with the bare skin underneath.

Morgan couldn't get enough of River. The warm woodsy scent of his skin. The searing heat of his hands gliding over her body, the low groans of pleasure against her lips… It all brought back a rush of memories that made her skin flush hot. Memories of their nights together. Of how much she needed him then, and now. It almost scared her how easily it came back after years of suppressing it. It made her worry that the temporary nature of their agreement might be harder to keep to as well. She wanted River, yes, but she couldn't let herself love him again. Not when he didn't know the truth.

Their lips didn't part until she felt him push her skirt up to her waist. "That should be enough," she whispered against his mouth. "For here." She added the last part, as though her hesitation was being naked at work where they might be caught, when in truth it was to keep as much of her body hidden from him as possible in the bright, late afternoon sunlight.

River nodded. Leaving her skirt where it was, he sought out her panties instead. His fingers hooked around the sides and tugged them down, slipping them past her patent leather heels and letting them fall to the floor like nothing more than the thin scrap of black lace they were.

He groaned aloud as he caught a glimpse of her bare flesh when he stood back up. She was quite disheveled with her blouse unbuttoned, her bra exposed and her skirt hiked up around her hips. Judging by his intense gaze and flexed jaw, he seemed to think she was the greatest thing he'd ever laid eyes on.

It made her feel sexy and desirable in a way that she rarely identified with. It had been a long time since someone had looked at her with such naked desire in his eyes. Since she'd *allowed* someone to look at her that way. The walls she built around herself after everything that had happened were high. Even with the anticipated prize of the Steele heiress on the other side, few men had tried to breach her protective barricades. Those who tried usually gave up before they reached her. And she was okay with that. It saved her the disappointment of finding they were just after her money.

River hadn't even thought twice about it before he'd scaled her walls, and there was a part of her that loved him for his reckless bravery where she was concerned.

But now his hesitation was starting to worry her. She'd expected him to dive back into devouring her, but he stopped, just looking at her. "I haven't changed my mind, River. I'm ready."

He nodded and smiled. Leaning in, he gave her a soft kiss and pulled back. "I'm ready, too. More than ready. That was just a sight I wanted to commit to memory. And now, first things first."

Morgan watched as he shuffled out of his suit coat and reached into his breast pocket for his wallet. He set it on the table and tossed the coat across the back of a nearby chair. He opened the wallet, pulling out a single condom before he cast the rest of it aside.

Of course, he would remember them this time. On their wedding night, he'd forgotten to buy some. They'd been so excited to steal away on their adventure that some of the details had been missed. Since they were technically married and holed up in their honeymoon cabin for the night, they decided that it was okay without them this one time. That ended up being a mistake. Morgan had had an IUD put in not long after Dawn passed away. She wasn't about to be caught in that position again.

River didn't know any of that. He just knew to plan better this time. Stepping back between her thighs, he put a condom on the table beside her bare hip. Then he wrapped one arm around her back and eased her backward until she was lying across the conference table. He leaned over her and unbuttoned the rest of her blouse. Running his hands over her breasts and down her rib cage, he stopped long enough to press a searing kiss on her sternum. The warmth of his touch against her skin heated her blood and ran through her veins as quickly as her racing heart could move it.

Morgan gasped and squirmed against the cold table. She longed to be enveloped by River's warmth, to chase away the chill, and he seemed content to tease her instead. When his hand sought out the moist heat between her thighs, she forgot about anything else. Her mind went blank to everything but the waves of pleasure that pulsated through her body. Her back arched off the table, her hands clawing futilely at the slick polished wood. There could be no question of her wanting him this time. Her body had given her away. He had her on the edge of climax and he'd barely touched her.

Then he pulled away again. She heard the clinking of River's belt and opened her eyes to see him undoing his zipper. Slipping on the condom, River gripped her hips and with his gaze fixed on hers, entered her in one slow stroke. Feeling the hard heat of him sinking into her welcoming body was a pleasure she'd missed for so long. She almost couldn't believe it was really happening. How many nights had she lain alone, wishing for one more kiss, one more embrace and then hating herself for still loving the man who had betrayed her and walked away? She wanted to pinch herself so she knew this was real.

Morgan pushed herself up upright, wrapping her

legs around his waist and her arms around his neck. She wanted to be as close to him as she could in this moment. Pressing her satin-covered breasts against the wall of his chest, she leaned in to whisper into his ear how much she needed him and nipped gently at his earlobe.

River shuddered then, gritting his teeth as he seemed to fight for control. It was a losing battle for them both. They'd both waited too long for this to take their time. He gripped at her back and pulled her so close to the edge she might have fallen without his support. Then he stopped holding back and gave her what she'd asked for. He filled her again and again, pounding hard into her willing body.

He seemed to know exactly what she needed from him and once again, she was on the edge of coming apart. She clung to him, gasping and whispering words of encouragement against his throat. "Please," she cried out as she neared her release, and he responded.

He pressed his fingers into the ample flesh of her hips and thrust until his legs began to shake. Morgan tensed and fell apart, shattering into her climax. It was only River that held her together, holding her tight until the last shudder rocked her body. It was then, with her cries finally silent, that River let go. He thrust hard and finished with a deep growl of satisfaction. Then, completely spent, he pulled them both down to the floor. Morgan fell to her knees straddling him as they collapsed into an exhausted, satiated pile on the expensive imported rug.

"So…" The younger man spun in his chair to face his webcam, a piece of licorice hanging out of the side of his mouth like a floppy red cigar. "I've got good news and bad news for you, Mr. Dalton."

Jade squeezed Harley's forearm a little tighter as they sat together in front of his laptop. She could tell he was getting irritated with his tech support team back in Virginia. He preferred to interface with his deputy of sorts, Isaiah Fuller, but he was tied up on another case the company was working. That meant the buffer between Harley and his team of geeks was gone.

They were supposed to be the best of the best, and yet it had taken them longer than he'd expected to run the backgrounds on his two primary suspects— Gregory Crowley and Robert "Buster" Hodges. Now that they had the information he needed, they seemed to be dragging it out.

Harley pinched the bridge of his nose. "Just tell me what you have, Eddie. I'm not in the mood for theatrics today."

The grin on the computer geek's face faded and

he quickly plucked the candy from his mouth and set it aside. "Yes, so at first glance, there wasn't much to look at. I've emailed you both their background checks, which came back pretty clean, all things considered. Not many leads there. The problem is that both of your guys have fallen off the face of the earth since the kidnapping. Neither are at their last known addresses with the DMV. They don't seem to be employed anywhere with any federal withholdings. If they are working, it's under the table."

"If we're on the right track, and I think we are, they have ten million dollars of mine and Steele's money. Why would they be working after a payday like that? How about their financial records? Any leads there?" Harley pressed. Jade watched as he reached for his phone and pulled up the background checks to scroll through while his employee reported his other findings.

"Not for Crowley. His only checking account was closed as overdrawn not long after the kidnapping. He doesn't have any credit cards or loans under his social security number. He's either living off the cash from the kidnapping, bought a new identity off the dark web or he's blown it all and is couch surfing somewhere."

"But you found something for Hodges?" Jade asked, hoping to turn the conversation toward better news. He had promised good news along with the bad after all.

"Yes, I did," Eddie continued. "There hasn't been any activity lately, but there was a purchase for an airline ticket a few days before the kidnapping. I figured that was him getting ready to run if all went well."

Jade felt her heart leap in her chest. This was the first real lead they'd had in a while and she was excited to hear the news. Being with Harley made her feel safer than she ever had before, but she had to admit that it was unnerving to know that her kidnappers were still on the loose.

"Were you able to get any details on the ticket?" Harley asked.

"It took a little digging, but yeah. According to the airline records, he bought a one-way ticket to Roatán, Honduras. He left the day after the ransom was paid, and then the credit card was paid off and the account was closed. The trail goes cold there."

Jade turned to Harley. "That's a start," she said hopefully, but the frown on Harley's face dashed her optimism a bit.

"It's a start, but with ten million dollars at their disposal, it's going to be hard to get much further. Like Eddie said, they could be under assumed names, living off cash. A couple fake ID's is all they would need. I'll have to see if I have any contacts in Central America that can help us out with the local authorities down there. It's a popular area for expatriates, so I'm not sure an older American would stand out much. But even if we find him, that only leads us to Buster."

"You don't think they're together?" Jade asked.

Harley shrugged. "Who knows? If it were me, I'd take my half and get as far away from the other guy as possible. Buster made the mistake of buying his ticket on his credit card, but Greg could've bought a bus ticket with cash going the other direction. Finding one doesn't mean we'll find the other."

Harley turned back to the webcam. "See if you can find any travel records for Greg. Even if he paid with cash, the airlines would have a record on their manifest. Check the trains and buses, too, just in case we get lucky. Whatever he could hop on and disappear. And also get me information on their families. Looking at their background checks shows they both have family living in the area, so get me their contact information. I find it hard to believe they'd both disappear without *someone* knowing where they are."

Eddie took a note down and nodded. "Will do, sir. Anything else?"

"Not for now."

The screen blacked out and Eddie's virtual presence in the room disappeared. Alone, Jade turned to Harley. "This is a real breakthrough, honey. I think we're on the right track."

He just sighed and leaned in to press a protective kiss on her forehead. "We're getting there. Slowly but surely. The people that hurt you can run, but they can't hide from me forever."

"Where are we going?" Morgan asked for maybe the tenth time since he picked her up from the office.

River smiled and kept his gaze fixed on the highway. "I told you when I asked you to pack a bag—and every time you've asked since then—*away*."

"*Away* isn't very helpful. I only packed a weekend bag. We aren't going far, are we? We're in the middle of a project, you know. It's not the best time for a spontaneous vacation."

He chuckled and kept driving, much to her continued irritation. "I'm aware of our responsibilities. But it's a Friday afternoon before Labor Day weekend and no one is doing anything on the housing project until Tuesday, including you and me. So we're going to my beach house for the long weekend and making the most of the time we have left together."

She turned to him with confusion etched between her eyebrows. "I didn't even know you had a beach house. I thought you just had the apartment in town."

"It's one thing to ask you to pack a bag to stay at my apartment for the weekend, but why would I go to the trouble of keeping the location a secret?"

"I don't know. You're complicated." She shrugged and looked out the window. "Where is your house?"

"You'll see." His response was answered with a groan from Morgan's side of the car.

Since their first sexual encounter in her office a few weeks prior, they'd met at his apartment every day for a long lunch of takeout and lovemaking. As he'd agreed to keep their relationship a secret, that didn't leave a lot of options for going out in public. His apartment was nearby and fine for what they needed most afternoons—he couldn't complain— but that wasn't what he had in mind for the long weekend.

No, he wanted to get Morgan away. Away from anything and everything that could distract her from enjoying herself—namely work and family. And then he was going to indulge at last.

For some reason, Morgan didn't seem to be interested in leisurely sex. Under the circumstances, a quick afternoon tryst made sense, but that was all she offered. Lunch was the only time she would agree to during the week, going back to her parents' mansion at night and always having things to do during the weekends, like gatherings with the Nolans or with

Jade to catch up on the investigation. He didn't begrudge her spending time with her family, but even when she did agree to come at lunch, she wanted him quickly and in dim lighting. Sometimes all the clothes came off, sometimes they didn't. But as soon as it was over, she was clothed and heading back to the office again.

He wasn't sure if she'd gotten more self-conscious about her body over the years, but he was tired of all that. From what he'd seen, there wasn't a thing to be embarrassed over.

If there was one thing his beach house offered, it was privacy. Even though his bedroom had a wall of windows overlooking the marshlands, there wasn't a neighbor in sight. They could make love on the beach, on the deck, in the pool, anywhere they liked without interruption. That was what he needed. This weekend he wanted to take his time, to worship her body and to become fully reacquainted with every inch of it. The weeks had gone by faster than he'd expected and he had a limited window of opportunity left with Morgan. The key ceremony was right around the corner. He intended to make the most of the time he had.

"The apartment is nice enough and close to work, but it's not exactly my idea of a real retreat. I only stay there when I'm working. With the traffic, going all the way to the beach and back can be a pain during the week. When I go out there, I want to stay for a while."

"I have to admit, a weekend at a beach house sounds lovely. I can't tell you the last time I did something like that. Probably last summer before Hurricane Florence hit. Did you have any damage from that?" she asked.

The storm had been a big scare for the Charleston area, bringing up fears of a repeat of the catastrophic Hurricane Hugo, but then Florence turned away and hit North Carolina instead. As a builder, he'd worried about the projects he had going on in the area, but when they were spared the worst of it, he sent some of his guys north to help with the cleanup efforts.

"Nothing too serious, thankfully. I knew what the risks were building on the coast here, so I designed the house specifically to withstand high winds and water surges. You can't live on the coast of the Carolinas without worrying about storms each season. Florence was its first real test and I'd say it passed with flying colors. I had to get some new patio furniture. That ended up who-knows-where. And I had to get the pool drained and cleaned. It was filled with mud and salt water and dead fish. That was a pretty big mess. But everything is back to normal now."

"It must've been fun to design and build a house just the way you wanted it."

Spying the sign for his turn, River got off the highway and headed toward Kiawah Island. "It was. That's what I've come to enjoy about construction. For the most part, I get to be in charge and things happen just the way I want them to."

Looking over at the beautiful woman in the car beside him, River wished he had that kind of oversight into every aspect of his life. The clock was ticking down on his time with Morgan. He didn't want to walk away from her this time with a single regret. He wasn't certain he would get his way, though.

Eight

River slid the large glass door aside and stepped out onto the patio with a glass of wine in each hand. Morgan was sitting on one of the outdoor couches, watching the sunset through the twisted oak and palmetto trees. The rear of his property was made up of several acres of undeveloped marshland that led to the sea, and sitting there, you could almost convince yourself you were the only person in the world.

"I can't believe this is your backyard," she said as she took the glass of chardonnay he offered.

"Yeah. When I saw this land, I knew it was where I wanted to build. It's not like I could find an existing house like this, anyway. It isn't exactly the historic Charleston design everyone wants down here. Or the typical beach house everyone rushes to rent over the summer. I like to think of it more as an overgrown tree house. What you'd expect a kid who grew up poor to blow his money on when he finally got some," he said with a smile. That was exactly what he had done. "What about you? What's your place in DC like?"

"Well, since I moved up there to go to college, I've been renting this little row house in Georgetown. It's two stories and narrow, not even a thousand square feet. It's more than enough for me, but it has no yard to speak of. I have a planter on the stairs to the front door and the plants in it are long dead, so I suppose it's just as well. I'm gone too much to really take care of a yard.

"If I decided to stay there, though, I'd probably buy a place that's a little bigger with private parking and perhaps a courtyard where I could put some chairs. I like the area. It's got that exciting college town vibe, plus it's close to the National Mall and all the events and museums there. One day, I hope to have free time to actually enjoy any of those things."

"You live in the middle of all that fun stuff, but you never play tourist?"

"No. I work too much. I'd like to go to the Smithsonian, though. They have a gemstone exhibit there with the Hope Diamond. There's also a necklace with a flawless pink diamond that I've seen pictures of. I fell in love with it and really want to see it in person someday. But even those priceless gemstones can't touch a view like this. This is like a painting in one of those museums I never visit."

River looked out to appreciate one of the perks of his home. The sky was starting to burn with orange and purples as the sun set. In the distance beyond the marsh, Folly Island was turning into a dark shadow. The temperature started to fall as the sun disappeared, giving the slightest chill to the ocean breezes that blew through the corridor where they were sitting. It was enough for Morgan to snuggle a little closer to him as they sat side by side and watched the sun set together.

"It really is amazing how much you've done with your life, River. I mean, did you ever dream that you'd have a home like this back when we first met?"

"Not at all. Most days I want to pinch myself. This place, my company, everything I've accomplished… I knew I had it in me, but I had no idea how to start. How do you build a company out of nothing? Especially since I had no education or savings. Construction was all I knew, but it's a big leap from the guy with a hammer to the CEO. Banks don't want to loan a kid like me the money it would take to get started. If it weren't for the money your father offered me that night, I don't know where I would be today. Certainly not the owner of my own com—"

"What?" She sat up abruptly, interrupting him.

River noted the slightly stunned expression on Morgan's face that was highlighted by the dwindling evening light. "I know it upset you that I took the money, but what else was I going to do? Turning it down seemed stupid. Having that cash gave me something to focus on instead of losing you."

"No," she shook her head. "I don't mean why did you take it. You would've been a fool not to take it. But you're saying that my father *offered* you the money? You didn't ask for it?"

He flinched at her words, the sound of them offensive to his ears. After his confrontation with Trevor, he had been fairly certain Morgan didn't know the truth about how the money had changed hands. It certainly explained her animosity toward him early on, but now she needed to know the truth. "Of course, I didn't ask for it."

He watched tears start to shimmer in Morgan's eyes and realized the version of the story she knew was far different. "After he put you in the car, he pulled a check out of his breast coat pocket and handed it to me. He said it was a little something to soothe my pride. What did your father tell you about it?" he asked. He wanted to know what kind of wicked picture Trevor had painted of him.

Instead of answering, she brought her hand up to cover her mouth. A tear broke free and ran down her cheek. He wrapped his arm around her and pulled her close. "Morgan, tell me," he insisted.

It took a few moments for her to compose herself, but after she'd wiped her eyes with a tissue, she stared down at her hands as she spoke. She seemed almost guilty, as though any of this was her doing. "My father told me that you asked for money to keep quiet about the marriage and cooperate with the annulment process. He basically called you a blackmailer who dropped me like a rock when money came into the picture. It broke my heart to think that you were so quick to demand a check and walk away."

River groaned and pulled her even tighter against him on the couch. That was what he'd been afraid of. "I let you go because that seemed to be what you wanted. When your father handed me the check, I was stunned. He told me not to be stupid and just take the money, but if he ever saw us together again, I'd have to repay every penny. He said I should use it to do something with my life, so that's what I did. I started my own company and built it into what I have today. To be honest, I never could've done it without that money to get me started, but a part of me wishes I hadn't taken it. Even if it meant I'd never have this house or the chance to see you again by collaborating on this project. The money didn't do anything to soothe my aching heart once you were gone."

"That sounds like something my father would say," she said with a soft sniff. "And it also seems like the kind of thing he would do, twisting his bribe into something that would ensure you stayed away and I hated you. He wanted to keep us apart and it worked. It worked too well. It made me so angry. It made me hate you so much that I never wanted to see or hear from you ever again. I thought I had given my heart away to someone who was just using me for money. And when I think about later on…" She broke into tears again.

River had never been a fan of Trevor Steele. But in this moment, seeing how brokenhearted Morgan was to learn the truth, he wanted to punch the man in the face. Was River so unsuitable for his daughter that it was worth hurting her so badly? He wasn't even sure she'd fully recovered from it. How could she learn to trust someone and be in any kind of serious relationship when her first one only taught her that men would use her for her money? Perhaps she would be willing to entertain something more than a casual fling if she hadn't felt so betrayed by love.

His love.

"River, I…" She stopped, her lower lip trembling slightly as she hunted for words.

"What is it?" He reached out and cradled her cheek in his hand.

She looked up at him for a moment with nothing less than fear reflecting in her moist green eyes. She was afraid of something. It wasn't him. Perhaps she was scared to share her feelings with him. That could be a scary prospect for her. Hell, it was scary enough for him. He'd felt a surge of joy run through him when he held her. An ache when they were apart. But with the key ceremony coming up, he didn't dare let himself consider what that meant.

"You can tell me," he said. He reached out and brushed a strand of her dark hair out of her face. "Anything."

Her lips parted to speak, but no sound came out. Morgan shook her head and let her gaze drop down to the collar of his shirt. "I'm sorry," she said at last. "I'm sorry for all of this."

"Don't be sorry. It's not your fault. You only knew what your father told you. I would've been pretty upset if I were in your position. No one wants to know that their love has a price."

"I know," she said with a sigh and melted against his chest. "This was my father's doing. And he and I are going to have a chat about it, soon."

"Please tell me you're looking for a job."

Greg peered over the top of the newspaper he was

reading to see his father shuffling into the kitchen. At nearly eighty years old, shuffling was as fast as he could move. His tongue was still as swift and deadly as it had ever been, though.

"Not exactly," he muttered back. He'd gazed over the classified ads, sure, but then he'd gotten bored and started reading the articles instead.

His father made a dismissive noise and disappeared back into the living room with a beer in hand to watch his evening game shows. Greg decided to ignore him. He'd found something far more interesting to focus on in *The Post and Courier*: the Steele Foundation was planning an event in two weeks. His eyes scanned the article quickly, trying to keep focused as the excitement built inside of him. This was his chance. He just knew it.

The article was focused mainly on the houses that they'd built in town and the needy families that had been chosen to receive the homes. It was a feel-good piece, but Greg didn't care about any of that. It was the last paragraph that really stood out. The family would be hosting a ceremony at their Mount Pleasant mansion to celebrate the completion of the homes and present the keys.

The last time he'd gone to the Steele mansion, he and Buster had waited outside for their chance to snatch up and ransom Jade Nolan. That wouldn't work this time, especially since he was on his own.

No, this time he needed to find a way to get *inside* the house. He imagined they had security at the door. The only people allowed in would be on their guest list. That meant the families and major donors only. That, and staff of course. It wouldn't be easy to get into the Steele mansion, but it could be done.

Thinking back to that night, Greg remembered that they'd pulled up alongside a white catering van near the rear of the house. They'd watched them carry out equipment and food, with easily a dozen servers in matching outfits going back and forth. The name and the company logo had been printed in black on the side of the van. It had had a smiley face with a bow tie, he was pretty sure. He tried to envision the logo in his mind, but the name of the company escaped him.

If the Steele family used the same catering company for each event, they might be the ones handling this upcoming party as well. For an event this large, he presumed they hired extra staff, perhaps from a temp agency. If he moved quickly, he might be able to get on board with the caterer for the event. That would give him unlimited access to the house, letting him move around easily among the guests and execute his plan without anyone questioning who he was and why he was there.

And what plan was that, exactly? He wasn't sure what he would do once he was inside the mansion, but he had some time to figure that out. First, he had to discover who would be catering the party.

Curious, he went to the cabinet where his father kept one of the last phone books in existence. Computers and smartphones were as alien to this household as robots and laser guns. He flipped through to the section of catering companies and found a large corner ad with the smiling face he remembered from the van.

Black Tie Affairs!

That was the company, he was certain of it. He glanced down at his watch. The library a few blocks away would be open for at least another two hours. If he went over there now, he could get on the computer and see about putting in an application with the company. His dad would be so pleased to know he was trying to get a job. Greg was certain this wouldn't be what he had in mind, though.

Slamming the phone book shut, Greg grabbed his keys and headed out the door to the library. His brain was spinning with ideas as he climbed into his van. He was almost giddy at the thought.

This was his chance to finally make an impact on the Steele family. Perhaps *literally*.

Morgan couldn't sleep.

After the wine and lovemaking, she should've

drifted off into a blissful slumber curled up at River's side, but it wasn't happening.

River was out cold. She could hear his rhythmic breathing in the bed beside her and she envied him. Of course, he had every reason to sleep well. His conscience was clean and the truth was finally out. Morgan, however, had a million different thoughts running through her mind.

Something about being here with him at his private retreat made it all too real. Spending the night together for the first time since they had dated as kids should've felt like an important milestone. They'd spent weeks taking long lunches together and avoiding any serious type of intimacy while they built the houses for her charity families. That was the way she had wanted it. That was the way she thought he wanted it, too. That was the smart thing to do. It wouldn't be long before they would be done building and she would return to DC. It was no time to fancy any type of real emotions where River and their future together was concerned.

But now, lying here, she was conflicted, not comforted, by his warmth beside her.

Maybe she liked it too much. Everything about being with River felt right, just like it had back in college. She could very easily let herself get lost in the fantasy of being with him. As though this were something real instead of a casual summer fling.

Deep down, she wanted it to be real. But she knew that was a dangerous idea. If she gave in to that dream, it would crush her just as badly as the first time she'd given in to her feelings for him.

That was because even with River beside her, his hand resting on her pillowcase, she could feel him slipping through her fingers. In some ways, he was already lost to her. The sooner she accepted that, the better.

The key ceremony was right around the corner. There was exactly two weeks until the event and if she intended for her relationship with River to continue beyond their agreed deadline the way she wanted it to, she had to take action.

Morgan had to tell River about their daughter.

The truth was like a dark cloud looming overhead. Anytime she thought she might see the sun, the clouds would roll in and remind her she was keeping the truth from him.

Talking about Dawn had never been easy. Perhaps because she'd never really gotten to talk about her. When the whole family either didn't know or was acting as though nothing had happened, you didn't have anyone to confide in.

Now that she needed to say something, she found she couldn't. She'd wanted to. Just hours before when she realized the truth about the money that River had been given, it had almost spilled out. In that moment, all she could think about was that she'd kept the truth from River all that time—hidden the pregnancy and everything that happened afterward—because of lies her father had told her.

Now she couldn't stop thinking about how things could've ended differently. The complications of the pregnancy might not have been avoided, but if she'd had River at her side as they went through the ups and downs of it, everything would've been different. She would've had her husband there to hold her hand and cry with her. He would've fought to have Dawn buried in a real graveyard where people would be able to see her tombstone and know she existed. Even the baby's name would've been different—Dawn Mackenzie Atkinson. Not Steele. Even though their marriage had been wiped from history, the baby would've had his name.

Telling him the truth back then would've been so much easier. Even with the animosity from her parents, telling River would've been the right thing to do. But telling him now? Somehow, it seemed like the one thing she had to do to make their relationship work was the one thing guaranteed to destroy it.

With a sigh, she rolled onto her back and looked up at the ceiling. The slanted roof had a skylight that gave her views of the night sky you couldn't get back in town with the light pollution there. She hoped for a shooting star to whiz by as she watched. Maybe then she could make a wish, and wish that all of this would work out at last with the man she loved.

Morgan cringed at the thought and the naïve stupidity that allowed her to think it. But she couldn't deny the truth. It was plain to see that she was in love with River again. Or more accurately, that she had always been in love with him. Even when she felt betrayed. Even when she was scared and alone and hated him for putting her in that position, she loved him.

Knowing he had never done anything to make him unworthy of her love made it that much harder to ignore. And that much harder to tell him the truth because he hadn't deserved the deception.

"Are you okay?"

Morgan turned her head to find River looking at her with concern lining his sleepy eyes. "Yeah, I'm fine."

"So you normally lie awake at night and stare intently at the ceiling?"

"I wasn't staring at the ceiling. I was looking up at the stars." She sighed and rolled over to look at him. "But no, it's not normal. I've just got a lot on my mind at the moment."

River pushed up onto his elbow and looked down at her. "I guess my plan to whisk you away to my peaceful, private retreat backfired. Do you want to talk about it?"

This was her chance. Here, in the dark, she could bare her soul. Confessions were always easier this way. And yet, maybe it was a bad idea. Maybe it was better to just enjoy this moment with River for what it was. To indulge the way she'd intended to when this first started, and then walk away from it.

Was it better to tell him the truth now and ruin everything? Right now, she had a lot on her mind, but she was comfortable and warm in River's bed. She could reach out and touch him if she wanted to. She could kiss him. Snuggle up against him. If she spoke up, she could very well ruin everything and end up waiting outside for an Uber at three in the morning to get back to Mount Pleasant.

Or was it a better idea to keep her mouth shut, let things come to their natural end and have this happy memory of their time together to cherish? The only way to truly keep the past in the past was to make sure her future didn't include River.

"Not really," she said, chickening out once again. "It's nothing you would want to hear about in the middle of the night."

"Try me."

"No. Just forget it. I don't want to waste another minute worrying about something I can't control." And she couldn't control it. Not really. She could tell him, but how he responded was on him. That's what scared her.

"Okay. Well, how about I help you forget about it?"

River grinned wide in the moonlight and she knew that this was the offer she would accept. To lose herself in loving him and trying to keep the memory in her heart so she wouldn't be too lonely without him.

Nine

Something was bothering Morgan, but once again, she wouldn't open up to him about it. River wasn't sure if she didn't trust him or if it was one of those damned Steele secrets holding her mind hostage. Either way, her stress was palpable and ruining the vibe of their weekend retreat.

So far things had been fine but hadn't exactly gone to plan. She was here in his bed, unable to flee back to the office or the mansion, but his indulgent fantasies were still out of reach. The lights were still dim or completely darkened when they made love.

And while they weren't fully or partially clothed, she had packed a wide array of lingerie.

Normally, River would find lingerie intriguing. Silky straps, lacy panels, strategic cutouts… There wasn't anything wrong with that. But on Morgan, it felt like a lacy barrier protecting her from something. Him, he supposed.

He'd offered to help her forget whatever was bothering her and the way she'd curled her leg around his hip seemed like an acceptance of his proposal. Her fingers were brushing over his beard and burying themselves in the thick waves of his hair. All signs pointed to her wanting him, and yet, as before, she was a little overdressed for the occasion. She'd put on a pale pink silk nightgown before she got into bed. It had to go. He'd just hold his breath to see if she stopped him.

He placed one open palm on her thigh and rubbed up her leg to her hip. River caressed the skin, skimming over her tummy and moving up beneath the chemise to cup one firm breast. He watched her reaction with curiosity, but so far, it was all okay.

Until he started pushing the gown up higher. That's when he felt her stiffening the way she had just before she bolted from that town house. He eased back, afraid to push her too far. They weren't in the middle of town where she could just jump up and leave. This time he was going to get to the bottom of it all.

"I need you to tell me exactly what it is that I'm doing that makes you nervous," he said.

Morgan bit at her lip as she pushed up onto her elbows. She gently tugged the gown back down as she shook her head. "It's nothing," she argued.

"Okay. Then let's take this thing off. It's in the way and I want to see you. All of you." River gripped at the hem to pull the silky slip of fabric over her head, but the fear in her eyes stopped him before she could argue.

"I'd rather not."

He sighed and leaned back. "I don't understand what you think you have to hide, Morgan. I could tell you that you're the most beautiful woman I've ever had in my bed. I could tell you that I've done nothing but fantasize about you for ten years—and in all those fantasies, you were completely naked. I'm not sure it would make a difference with you, though."

"Fantasies aren't reality. I'm not nineteen anymore."

"I don't want you to be nineteen. I want *you*. Right now. Just as you are. And I want you to trust me when I say that I mean it. I don't know what you could possibly be hiding. Did you get an ugly tattoo? Grow a big hairy mole? A gnarly scar? None of that matters to me. You're beautiful, Morgan. Every inch of you."

Her brow knit together in thought as she considered his words. "Give me a minute," she said at last.

He considered arguing but thought better of it. If she needed a little bit of time to be comfortable with the idea, he shouldn't push her. "Okay."

Morgan left the bed, rummaging through her luggage for a moment and then disappeared into the bathroom. River laid back against the pillows and stared up at the skylight. A moment later, he saw a streak of light cross the sky. Maybe he would get his wish tonight and Morgan would stop holding back. The clothes and the lighting seemed like they were just a physical manifestation of the way she was resisting her feelings for him. He'd hoped getting her here away from the city and the Steeles might help.

When the bathroom door opened, all River could see was the nude silhouette of Morgan against the bright backlighting. The nightie was gone, with all of her curves on display. He could tell she was topless. The natural movement of her full breasts and their taut nipples were visible as she turned to face him, even from a distance. But as his eyes adjusted to the light, he noticed that she wasn't entirely naked. Even after their discussion.

Morgan crossed the room, leaned over to the nightstand and flipped on the small lamp there. The light bathed the room in a golden glow that wasn't too bright, but it was more light than he'd seen her in, as yet. Now he could see that she had on some clothing, but it was hard to complain about her choice of outfit. She had on a fire-engine red satin garter belt with red and black lace that stretched over her hips and tummy. The garters stretched down her creamy thighs and each clasp had a silk rosette that held up a sheer pair of black stockings. A hint of her bare skin was visible beneath the edge of the lace as she moved, and he was pretty sure there were no panties beneath the garter belt.

Then Morgan surprised him by turning around to give him the full view. Apparently, it wasn't shyness that kept her partially covered. In the back, the lingerie had little more than a thin belt and another set of garters holding up the stockings. The plump curve of her bare ass was gloriously on display, confirming his suspicions about her missing panties.

"Damn," he whispered as she turned back to face him. If she felt the need to wear *something*, River had to admit it was a great choice.

She pulled back the covers and slipped into the bed. "Is this okay?" she asked. "There shouldn't be anything in your way."

River could hardly speak for the lump in his throat. He only nodded and reached for her. "Come here," he said at last with a rough voice.

Morgan immediately curled beside him, letting River cover every inch of her body with his own. He ran his hands over her stockings, loving the feel of them against his rough skin. She didn't hesitate to part her silk-clad thighs as he moved higher, letting him seek out her heat with his hand.

She gasped and arched her back off the bed as he gently stroked her center. He teased at it at first, applying more pressure gradually until she was pressing her hips against his hand. He slipped one finger, then another inside of her, grinding harder until she was panting and squirming anxiously beneath him.

"I need you now, River," she cried. "I don't want to come without you."

He stilled his hand, considering sending her over the edge anyway, but opted to give her what she wanted. With a condom in place, he nestled between her thighs and found his home there. He bit his lip and surged forward until he was buried deep inside her. He closed his eyes and savored the feeling of her heat wrapped around him. The soft stockings rubbing against his hips as she pulled up her legs to cradle him, the rough tickle of her lace garter belt against his stomach.

Even with that last scrap of clothing left behind, it seemed like a victory. He'd never felt closer to Morgan than he did at that moment.

She must have felt the same way, because they

moved together as though thcy were one person. River refused to rush this time, slowing the pace to taste her mouth, her throat and her breasts. Tonight, they had all the time in the world together to enjoy this. He reveled in the sound of Morgan's soft cries and the press of her fingertips into his shoulder blades. After the last few weeks together, he could even feel her release building up inside as her muscles tensed around him and her breath moved rapidly in her chest.

"River," she gasped with an edge to her voice.

She was so close. He knew she would be after he'd taken her so far before. This time he wasn't going to stop until she was screaming his name. "Don't hold back, baby," he whispered against the outer shell of her ear. "Just let it happen."

River was talking about more than just her orgasm. He wanted her to stop resisting all of this. Maybe she felt like she had good reasons to hold back her feelings for River, but he didn't want her to fight it anymore. He wanted this moment to last. Beyond tonight, beyond the weekend, beyond the key ceremony. He wanted to give this a real try without the interference of anyone else.

They deserved a second chance. A real chance, not just some fling to relive their youth and soothe their past wrongs. They both knew it meant more than that. He was lost the moment he laid cycs on her again. All the old feelings, good and bad, had rushed to the surface. With most of the bad set aside, he was tired of fighting the good.

"Yes, River!" she shouted to the empty room, clinging to his shoulders as her body was rocked with the spasm of her release. "Yes!" she cried again and again until she stilled beneath him.

It was only then that River let himself finish. He buried his face in her throat and thrust into her until he unraveled with a low groan of pleasure.

After a moment, River rolled onto his back to catch his breath. He could get used to being woken up like that more often. He stumbled into the bathroom to clean up, and when he returned a moment later, he found that Morgan had changed back into the silky chemise he'd banished from the bed earlier.

With a sigh, he climbed back under the covers, wanting so badly to say something about the outfit. Instead, he snuggled up with her and decided to enjoy their night for what it was. They'd made progress. Baby steps, but progress.

"So tell me," he said, as they were on the edge of sleep. "It's an awful tattoo you're hiding, isn't it? Do you have Kermit the Frog on your hip bone or something? Property of Big Jim?"

He was answered only with a fluffy pillow straight to the face.

"Good night, River," was all she said.

"Good night," he replied with a chuckle. He pulled her close against him and drifted off into a contented sleep.

Normally, when Morgan worked at Steele headquarters, she tried to stay as far away as she could from the executive suites. That was the turf of her father, brothers and others entrusted with the day-to-day running of Steele Tools. There, they discussed and worried about things she couldn't care less about—like whether moving their manufacturing facility to China would improve their bottom line, or if a hammer looked better with the traditional Steele red or exciting new yellow rubber grips.

Tools were the family industry and she reaped the benefits of it, but that didn't mean she had to live and breathe it the way the others did. In fact, if her father hadn't indulged her in creating a charitable branch she could run, she wouldn't have worked for the company at all. Several people in the family had started in the company and branched off into careers in politics or kicked off their own start-ups. Morgan felt like she would be one of those who eventually stepped out of the tool business. Into what, she had no idea.

But Tuesday morning, after her long weekend at River's place on Kiawah Island, she marched down the hallway toward the executive offices like a woman on a mission. She ignored everyone she passed on the way to her father's office. It was early, not even eight o'clock yet, but she knew he would be there. Her father had spent the majority of his life in this office. If he wasn't at home, he was in his executive chair, wheeling and dealing.

His administrative assistant hadn't come in yet, and for that, she was thankful. One less roadblock. She glanced through the glass of his office wall long enough to confirm he was there and alone, then she barged inside.

Her father shot up in surprise, nearly spilling the coffee he was sipping all over his keyboard. "Morgan!" he declared, before gently setting the coffee aside. "Is something wrong?"

"Yes. I have something I have to ask you and I need you to be honest with me."

Trevor cocked his head curiously and gestured to the guest chair. "Okay. Why don't you sit down, sunshine, and we can talk it all out."

She winced at the sound of her pet name. She was not in the mood to be Daddy's little girl. She was mad at him and she didn't want him clouding her feelings with things like that. Still, she sat down in the chair, hovering on the edge and refusing to relax into the soft leather. "I had a discussion with River recently. He mentioned how he used the money you bribed him with to start his company.

That sounds a little bit different from the version of events you told me."

"Bribe is a strong word, Morgan." Trevor smiled at his daughter indulgently, but she wasn't going to let him sweet-talk his way out of this. It was her life he was toying with. She wasn't a chess piece to be moved around at his will.

"Dad, this is no time for semantics. Did River demand the money to go or did you offer it to him?"

Trevor sat back in his chair and sighed. "What does it matter? He took the money, didn't he? That's the important part, isn't it?"

"No, it isn't. I don't blame him for taking what was offered. What else did he have after you stole me away? What's important is that you made me believe that he had demanded that money to go away quietly. You told me that you had to pay him off to keep him from stalling the annulment and demanding a part of my estate since I was too naïve to get a prenuptial agreement. You told me he threatened to go to the newspapers about our affair if you didn't write him a check on the spot. None of that was true, was it?"

Trevor watched her for a moment, the muscles in his jaw tensing. "No, it wasn't true," he admitted at last. "I told you that so you'd keep away from him. He wasn't the right boy for you, but you were too blinded by young love to see it. I offered him the money in the hopes he'd take it and disappear. And he did. So things worked out in the end, didn't they? He's a success. You're doing well. No harm, no foul."

She shook her head. "I can't believe this. When he told me about the money, there was a part of me that was certain this was just his way of getting me to move past it. But River was telling the truth. You bribed him, and then made me think he was just a gold digger using me to get to my money."

"I thought it was for the best, sunshine. It was a story so awful that it would make the break clean and you wouldn't try to run back to him when I wasn't looking."

"For the best? Daddy, do you realize what you did? You didn't just break up a pair of young, foolish lovers. You broke my heart when you told me that. You made me believe that no man could ever love me just for me, that my money would always be a factor when a man showed an interest in me. It made me so suspicious that I stopped trusting people. All these years… After everything that happened…"

Trevor frowned as she spoke, but he didn't interrupt. "Morgan, I never realized it had that kind of impact on you. I only wanted you to marry someone who was worthy of you."

"River was worthy. He was worthy in more ways than I can count. He wasn't rich, but he was a good person and he loved me. So tell the truth—when you say worthy, you mean rich."

He sighed. "When you have the kind of money our family has, it's not unheard of for people to be targeted romantically. How was I to know if River was sincere or not?"

"It would've helped if the first words you spoke to him weren't, 'Get your hands off my daughter and put on some clothes.'"

Trevor leaned closer and cocked a brow at her. "It also would've helped if I had met my future son-in-law before he was my son-in-law, Morgan. By secretly eloping, it seemed like you had something to hide."

"I did. I was hiding him from you, because I knew that you wouldn't allow us to get married." Morgan's gaze dropped sadly to the hands she had folded in her lap. "You've controlled every aspect of my life since I was a child. The moment I tried to live my own life as an adult, you shut it down."

"You got married, Morgan. This wasn't a nose piercing or some other type of harmless youthful rebellion. You married a boy you'd known for less than three months. Without your family. Without a prenuptial agreement. Letting you live your own life was starting out as a disaster. You were only nineteen years old."

Morgan's head snapped up as his words fanned

the fire of anger heating her cheeks. "Stop it right there. Stop twisting this conversation into a lecture about what you think I did wrong with my life. We're here to talk about what you did. You *lied* to me. You manipulated my feelings. I'm almost thirty years old and sometimes I think you're still pulling the strings of my life like I'm some marionette puppet."

"I think that's a little overdramatic, Morgan."

"Maybe, but I'm allowed to feel however I want to feel. You're not in charge of that." She took a moment to collect her thoughts and figure out what she wanted to say to him. "I think that perhaps having you as my father and my boss has given you too much control in my life. Perhaps some space would be healthy."

Trevor chuckled dismissively at her words. "You can't quit being my daughter."

"Technically, I could. I'm sure the Nolans would be happy to see more of me. I haven't gotten to spend as much time with them as I'd like to, but I'm pretty certain they would never tell me who I could love or decide who was good enough for me. But I couldn't do that to the rest of the family. Or to you, no matter how badly you've hurt me, Daddy. But I can quit my job."

That caught his attention. He sat upright in his chair, no doubt thinking of all the loose ends she would leave behind if she walked out the door at that exact moment. "Are you serious?"

Morgan took a deep breath and nodded. "Yes. But don't worry, I'll finish this year's project. It's too late in the game to turn it over to someone else. But after the key ceremony is over, you can consider this my notice."

Her knees were shaking as she pushed herself up from the chair and turned her back on her father. She tried to walk to the door without losing her cool and made it as far as grasping the handle when her father spoke again.

"Does he know about Dawn?"

Morgan froze on the spot, her hand gripping the doorknob for support. She couldn't make herself turn around or face him, because they both knew the answer to his question was no.

"You kept that from him, didn't you? Because you thought it was for the best. That he would be hurt by the truth."

She felt her father's presence behind her as his hand came to rest gently but firmly on her shoulder. She didn't flinch away from his touch, as even in this moment, it was a comfort to have him there. He was always there for her, even when she thought she didn't need him.

"You justified keeping your daughter a secret in

your mind, but if he found out about her now, don't you think he would be angry with you?"

"Yes." Somehow, she knew he would be. She had punished him for a crime he hadn't committed and now they would all suffer for it.

"Now you see where I'm coming from, sunshine. I'm sorry that what I did hurt you. It was the last thing I wanted to do. But we all make choices and sometimes the right answer isn't so easy to come by. Sometimes we end up hurting the ones we love in an attempt to protect them."

She did understand. She didn't want to, but she did. There was a part of her that had kept the truth about their daughter from River to protect him. But she'd also been angry with him. Now that those excuses were gone, what was keeping her silent? It was knowing that finding out the truth now would only hurt him. And that he would blame her.

"Do you think he'll ever be able to forgive me?" she asked quietly, the words barely a whisper.

The hand on her shoulder tightened into a gentle squeeze of support. "For your sake, I hope so, honey."

Ten

Greg straightened the bow tie provided by his temporary employer and took a deep breath. This was it. Weeks of planning and years of frustration were going to culminate tonight. Not in a payoff, no, but in some sweet revenge.

As he carried around a tray of full champagne flutes, he noticed how the rich partygoers hardly paid any attention to him. Like he wasn't good enough to be acknowledged as a simple waiter. They saw the champagne, though. They snatched that off the tray and continued their conversations, dismissing him once they had what they wanted.

It took everything he had not to say, *You're welcome*, in a mocking tone. He only had to hold it together for a little bit longer.

As the last drink was taken, Greg turned back to the kitchen where the catering team was working. Black Tie Affairs had hired on a team of servers for the event with surprisingly few background checks. They hadn't even realized his ID was a fake. They thought his name was Carl. And they hadn't really looked at him, either. He was just there for the grunt work.

Boy, were they all in for a surprise. If they'd paid more attention, they would've noticed the strange boxes he unloaded into the ballroom with the rest of the catering equipment. Soon, those carefully placed explosives hidden beneath the linen table skirting would rip this ballroom and everyone nearby into tiny pieces. And that waiter, the one they never even looked at, would disappear in the chaos as a presumed victim of the blast. They wouldn't be able to pick "Carl" out of a lineup. Their own arrogance would see to it that he would get away scot-free.

"Carl, take this bag of trash out, please."

With a sigh, Carl set aside his tray and grabbed the heavy sack of cooking scraps. He went out the back door and tossed it into the dumpster the Steeles had had delivered for the event. As he stood out there, he looked at the sea of expensive cars parked across the lawn. He couldn't afford the tires on one of those vehicles. He was done. Done with these rich, entitled people getting everything and him getting nothing.

It would be easy to just walk away now and listen to the explosions and the screams as he disappeared into the night. But he wanted to see it. For once in his life, he wanted to watch one of his plans be executed without a hitch. So he went back inside.

"Carl, take this tray of canapés out, please." The head caterer slid a platter of tiny, fancy little foods toward him. He picked up the tray out of habit and carried it with him into the ballroom.

Instead of going into the crowd, however, he eased back into a safe corner, far from the bombs. He set the tray of food on a table and reached into his pocket for the detonator. He wanted to wait for the perfect moment. He took one last look around the room... A crowd had gathered onto the dance floor. That would be perfect. He thought of his sister...of his mother...and then he placed his thumb over the button and took a deep breath.

It was done. The keys were in the hands of three deserving families and instead of feeling happy or even relieved, River almost felt sick to his stomach.

He knew it wasn't the champagne. As he stood at the edge of the ballroom and watched the others, he could see that everyone else was drinking the same bubbly beverages without ill effects. Of course, they weren't on the verge of losing the most important person in their life, either.

River tried to focus on something else. It was supposed to be a joyous event after all. The Steele mansion was once again draped in expensive fabrics and flower arrangements. They had gone all out, as usual. The ballroom was filled with people in formal attire, there to celebratè how wonderful they were for contributing to a good cause. Tonight, they'd gotten their big payoff—celebrating and applauding as they gave out the house keys to the needy families, and consuming a down payment's worth of champagne and canapés.

Like the fund-raiser, the event was a little over-the-top for River. He'd be just as happy to skip the party and put that money toward the houses or another good cause. Of course, the Steeles thought it was important to have this special and exciting night for everyone, but as someone who had received charity in the past, it made him uncomfortable. Not everyone wanted a light shone on the fact that they needed help to get by.

Thankfully, the families seemed comfortable enough. They were easy to spot in the crowd, wearing their Sunday finest for the black-tie event. It wasn't too much to suffer through to get a brand-new house in the end.

This was at least a smaller event than before. Now he could easily find Morgan in the crowd. She was speaking with an older couple who had to be her biological parents. He hadn't been introduced to the Nolans, but it was obvious she was a younger version of Carolyn Nolan, with the same creamy complexion, curvy figure and luxurious shiny dark hair.

It was hard to focus on anything other than Morgan, however. Her scarlet-red gown fit her like a glove. It was one shouldered, leaving a single collarbone and arm gloriously bare. It bunched around the waist, clinging to her rounded hips, and fishtailed to the floor in a crimson train that trailed behind her. She looked stunning—every bit the Steele heiress, despite her newfound pedestrian roots. The color alone was enough for her to stand out among the darker hues of the other partygoers, even though he could've found her without it. She was like a shining beacon that directed him home.

It seemed like a lifetime since he'd walked into the ballroom and laid eyes on Morgan for the first time after all those years apart. Since then, they'd spent weeks in each other's arms. They'd worked through a lot of their old baggage. Truths had come to the surface, healing old wounds they'd both carried through their years apart.

River knew they'd discussed their little dalliance only lasting through to tonight, and they hadn't mentioned otherwise, but he couldn't walk away from Morgan when it was over. She turned and looked at him then, a soft smile curling her cherry-red lips. He smiled back and felt his chest tighten as though she'd reached into his rib cage and clutched his heart in her fist. No. He wasn't giving up on her again. It didn't matter what her father or anyone else had to say about it. He would tell her so when he got the chance, but so far tonight she'd been a crimson bumblebee, flitting around the room in her official capacity for the event.

Finally, she broke away from the conversation with the Nolans and headed in his direction. "Good evening, Mr. Atkinson," she said with a smile.

"Miss Steele. You throw a lovely party," he said, mimicking her polite and formal greeting. Even now, weeks later, she wanted the two of them to remain a secret. So it wouldn't be ruined. Or something like that. Now he wasn't so sure it didn't have more to do with her father's disapproval. Trevor Steele could certainly ruin things if he wanted to. He'd caught the man's icy stare across the ballroom a few times, but they hadn't spoken since that afternoon in the lobby of Steele Tools' corporate offices.

"Thank you." She glanced around at the mingling crowds. "I wish more people were dancing, but it seems to be going well, otherwise."

"I always believe in leading by example." River

reached out a hand to escort her onto the mostly empty dance floor. He knew it was a dangerous offer and judging by the wary look in her eye, so did she. They'd spent the last few weeks keeping their relationship in the shadows. To take a step out onto the dance floor together would be to shine a bright light on the two of them. Sure, it might just seem like a polite dance to anyone watching, but they would know better. And so would her father.

He was pleased and a little surprised when she placed her soft hand into his. He gave her a smile of encouragement as they stepped out onto the dance floor. He put one hand gently on her waist and kept a polite distance as they started to sway slowly to the music being played by the string quartet nearby. It seemed to do the trick. Within a few minutes, there were half a dozen other couples out there with them, including the Nolans.

"See?" he said. "Now people are dancing."

"Thank you," she said, although she seemed a little nervous. She kept glancing around as they danced, only making eye contact for a split second before anxiously glancing around again.

"You look beautiful tonight," he said. "That color on you is stunning. Reminds me of that lacy little thing you wore at the beach house."

That seemed to finally bring a genuine smile to her face and a little color to her cheeks. "Thank you,

River. I can get used to you in that tuxedo as well. You've come a long way from the jeans and T-shirt you were wearing when I hit on you in Five Points."

River chuckled at the mention of the downtown bar district near USC where he'd first met Morgan. Even that first time, he was able to pick out her light in the crowd like a neon sign. "I'm pretty sure *I* hit on *you*."

"You're probably right. I remember thinking it was pretty cocky of you to approach a group of girls and ask to buy me a drink. We were an intimidating crew."

"It didn't matter. You could've been surrounded by a pack of angry dogs and I would've gone straight to you. I couldn't help myself."

His gaze fell on the long elegant line of her neck exposed by her hairstyle and the cut of her gown. The thick dark waves were twisted on top of her head with a few soft tendrils kissing her skin the way he longed to. He spoke up to keep his lips occupied with another task. "Morgan, I need to tell you something."

She looked up at him with wide green-gold eyes. "What is it? Is something wrong?"

"Well, yes and no. I just needed to say…to tell you…that I lied."

She frowned as she looked up at him. "You lied? About what?"

"I didn't realize I was lying at the time, but when I said that I would be okay with this ending tonight… I'm not okay with it. I want more than just a casual fling with you, Morgan. I want to be with you. Publicly. For the long term."

"River, I—"

He held up his hand to stop her protest before returning it to her hip. "I want you to look your father in the eye and tell him that we're together. And that it's serious. Because it is, despite our best intentions. At least, this is serious for me." He considered saying more. To tell her that maybe he was falling in love with her again, but the conflicted look in her eyes held his tongue for now. "It is serious for you?"

She glanced around the room again before she looked up at him. "Yes, but…can we talk about this after the party? This is a little heavy for the dance floor."

He swallowed his disappointment and nodded stiffly. "Sure." He was certain she felt more for him than she was letting on, but she was afraid. Afraid of telling Daddy that she'd fallen into the same trap a second time with an unacceptable boy. Afraid of causing a scene at one of the family events and being the subject of cruel whispers. "Just, uh, forget I said anything. It was stupid of me to even bring it up tonight with everything else going on."

"No, River. I don't want to forget about it. I just want to—"

Her words were cut off by a sudden blast from the far side of the room that rocked the entire house.

It was absolute chaos after the explosion. After a large boom, the left side of the ballroom exploded into a fireball. Chairs flew across the room as the sound of shattering glass and horrified screams followed it. People started yelling and scattering around the house.

Morgan hardly knew what to do as the thick clouds of black smoke filled the room. All she could think about was who was in the ballroom. Who had been closest to the blast? Had it been one of her brothers? Her parents? The Nolans? Did she just lose the chance to get to know her birth parents? Was it one of the families who had come to get the keys to their new home? Her heart was breaking in her chest as she struggled to see if anyone was hurt.

River was more focused. He took Morgan's hand and led her from the room as quickly as they could make it. They went the opposite direction of the crowds, heading for the back door and the gardens beyond it. They ran a safe distance across the lawn, collapsing together on a stone bench on the far side of the gardens.

Morgan's lungs burned and her eyes stung from

the soot, but she wanted to go back inside. She wanted to help. But River kept his firm grip on her. She finally gave up, dropping her face into her free hand with a choking sob. "What happened? I didn't see it. Was it a gas leak?"

"I doubt that. It seemed more deliberate to me."

"Who would do such a thing?" she asked. To set off a bomb at a party where needy families were celebrating—that was despicable.

"I don't know," he said. "But they'll be caught and brought to justice. If I know anything about Trevor Steele, it's not to cross him. He will take care of it."

"If he can. What if he…?" She lost the words as she thought about what could've happened to the people in her life. They could be hurt. Or dead.

He pulled her to his chest and she rested her wet cheeks there against the lapel of his tuxedo. When she opened her eyes again, her gaze fell to the tiny marble grave marker that sat just beyond the bench to their left. To escape the danger, River had managed to lead her someplace far, far more treacherous than the burning house. She was frozen for a moment, wondering if perhaps the darkness would hide what she plainly recognized on sight.

"Everything will be okay," he assured her. Then she felt him stiffen against her and she knew that something had changed.

Morgan was afraid to breathe. Afraid to move. Perhaps he hadn't seen it. Or if he had, didn't understand the significance of what he was looking at. It was just a name and a date after all. A date that was far too soon for a child of theirs to be born.

"Morgan?" he asked.

She could feel his fingers start to press more insistently into her upper arms. "Yes?"

"What am I looking at?"

She squeezed her eyes tightly shut for a moment and then forced herself to sit up. This was it—the moment she'd been avoiding for ten years. That explosion had driven them straight to the heart of her darkest secret.

"Dawn," he read aloud when she didn't immediately answer him. "I remember that you said you liked that name back when we'd fantasized about our future children. Wasn't it your grandmother's name?"

"My great-grandmother," was all she could say.

When she looked at River, she could see the change in him. Every muscle in his body was tensed, his jaw set like stone as he looked down at Dawn's tombstone. A million different things started running through her mind. Reasons. Explanations. And yet, she couldn't even think of where to start.

His hands left her body then, leaving cold spots on her skin. She sat up, longing for his support now when she needed it the most. He still didn't look at her. She was certain nothing—not even the screaming and sirens in the distance—could tear his attention away from the tiny marble plaque.

"Tell me."

Morgan sat up straight, the tears starting to roll down her face as she began the story that was so long overdue. "That is where my father buried the urn that holds the ashes of my daughter. *Our* daughter."

"We had a daughter." It was a statement, not a question.

"Yes. I found out I was pregnant a few weeks after our wedding when I'd returned to campus. I was in denial for so long I didn't tell anyone. I was so hurt, so confused by everything that had happened. I thought I still had time to figure things out, and then I started having complications. It was too soon for the baby to come, but the doctors didn't have much of a choice."

She didn't want to lose him in the details about how sick she'd gotten and how she'd been at risk herself. Not now. Maybe later, once the shock of it all settled and he could understand everything she'd been through. "The doctors tried so hard, but I lost her only a few hours after she was born. They took her directly to the NICU after she was delivered, and I never even got to hold her."

"That makes two of us," he said with a cold edge to his voice.

This was the response she'd been so afraid of. The words were like sandpaper across her already raw wounds. They'd really never healed, but having River back in her life had just ripped it all open again.

"How could you keep this from me, Morgan?"

"After everything that happened between us? I didn't even know where to start. I was so angry with you then. I thought you'd extorted money from my father and abandoned me. Even though you didn't know about the baby, I think I blamed you for walking away while I dealt with everything by myself."

"I didn't walk away."

"I know that now, but back then I was reeling from everything going wrong in my life. I was scared and hurt and I didn't know what to do. And then once I lost Dawn, I thought maybe it was best that I not tell you. What good would come of telling you we had a daughter when she was already gone? I know I made the wrong choice, and I'm sorry."

"And now?" River asked, finally turning to look at her with a cold, impassionate stare. "I understand that back then things between us were complicated. But what about now? When you knew the truth about the money and what your father did? After we made love? All the times we were alone and talking about our lives? You've had a million chances to tell me over the last few months."

"I know. Believe me when I tell you how much I've wrestled with this knowledge. It lingered on the tip of my tongue every time we were together, but how could I say the words? The longer I waited, the harder it became. She was already gone. And when I realized how I felt about you, I… I didn't know how to… I thought you'd hate me for it."

Morgan stopped short of telling River that she loved him. It was true, but she didn't want to taint that moment with this. It would fall on deaf ears, and she didn't want to be accused of manipulating his emotions.

"And if the baby hadn't come early and everything had worked out okay…would you have told me about her then? Would you have given her up for adoption without ever giving me the chance to have a say in it? Or would I have run into a child with my eyes as she played here in the backyard?"

"Of course, I would've told you," she said, although she wasn't truly certain as she spoke the words aloud. She'd never gotten that far in the decision-making process, but he didn't need to know that.

"Dawn Steele," he repeated their daughter's name from the marble slab. "You didn't even give her my name. You hid her away in this dark corner of the yard like all the other family secrets. It's like she and I never existed in your lives."

"River, I—"

"Just don't." River turned away from her and looked out at the chaos unfolding around them. There were police and firemen all over the property with red lights and flames lighting up the sky. He watched it all dispassionately, as though it were not the scene of a terrorist act so much as a welcome distraction from the drama of his own life.

He wouldn't look at her and in that moment, that was all Morgan wanted. She was desperate to connect with him and explain everything she'd been through, but he wasn't going to listen to anything else she had to say.

"It looks like they have someone in custody," he said at last.

Morgan looked in the direction of his gaze, seeing a wiry older man facedown in the grass with Harley Dalton sitting on his back. The police were in the process of cuffing the man she didn't recognize, although he appeared to be wearing the same uniform as the caterers her office had hired for the party.

River stood up. "It looks like they've got everything under control here. You should be safe, now."

"You're leaving?" Morgan asked. She felt like

her heart was slowly being ripped from her chest the farther he moved away from her.

He nodded. "I think it's for the best," he said.

Morgan sat helpless, watching as the man she loved, the man she'd hurt, walked across the lawn and out of her life. She feared that it might be for good.

Now she knew how he had felt.

Eleven

Morgan had all her clothing laid out across the bed. Normally, she would stay around for a few weeks after the key ceremony to visit friends and actually enjoy some time back in Charleston instead of just working. She should spend more time with the Nolans, thankful they were unharmed in the explosion and she had the chance. But this year, for obvious reasons, she was ready to go back to DC. Some might call it running away. She preferred to think of it as getting her life back to normal.

If it ever had been normal.

Normal people didn't have a weirdo try to blow

them up at a party. The cops were long gone now, but the plastic tarps still covered the gaping hole in the side of the ballroom and the police tape blocked the room off from the rest of the house. Thankfully, the fire had been contained there and the rest of the house was still livable, but it was a reminder of the explosion and everything that had followed it.

She wanted to head back to her Georgetown town house. It wasn't tainted with the good and bad memories of River and everything else that had happened. It was a clean slate; her whole life there was. And after the last few months, she was desperate for that kind of refuge.

Morgan walked over to her closet and grabbed a handful of shoes to carry back to the bed. When she looked up, she saw her father lurking in the doorway to her room. She was startled by his sudden appearance. He normally didn't stray into the children's wing of the mansion, especially now that they were no longer children.

"Did you need something?" she asked as she dumped the armful of shoes onto the duvet.

Trevor narrowed his gaze at her for a moment and then shook his head. "I was just watching you. I'm surprised you're packing already. Is this about the explosion? They have the man who did it in custody. It's perfectly safe to stay."

"No, it's not about that." Morgan shrugged and

picked up a pile of folded clothes to put in her suit-case. "It's just time to go. There's no reason to hang around. I don't live here, after all."

"I forget sometimes," Trevor said with a rueful smile. "I think it's easier to let myself believe that you're still my little girl with your pigtails and baby dolls."

"It's been a long time since I've sported pigtails, Daddy. I'll be thirty in less than a week."

Trevor crossed his arms over his chest and sighed. "I know. And if I hadn't already realized you were grown-up, seeing you at the key ceremony the other night would've made it indisputable."

She wasn't sure what he meant by that. "I was dressed up the same as I have been at any of those parties you've thrown."

"It was different this time. Maybe it was seeing you with River."

She cast a quick glance at her father before reaching for a pair of Jimmy Choo heels to slip into a protective bag for safekeeping. "I didn't think you'd noticed. There wasn't any yelling about it, at least. In fact, you've hardly mentioned River's presence all summer."

"After I ran into him in the lobby and realized why he was here, I decided that maybe this time I needed to stay out of it. Things seemed to be going well for the charity project, and you made it clear to me that my help only hurt the last time. It was the right choice. The project was amazingly successful this year, and you two seemed pretty cozy together at the key ceremony. Watching you dance, I'd dare say something serious had sparked up again."

"Well, you don't need to worry about that," Morgan snapped. She focused on her packing, placing things into her bag at an accelerated pace to avoid thinking anymore about River.

"I wasn't worried. I've actually been giving it a lot of thought. You two seem like you're in a better place to try a relationship. You're older, more established. I'm not going to interfere this time, is what I'm trying to say."

Morgan couldn't help a bitter chuckle. Of course, her father would finally approve of River once it was over between them. "That's good to know, but it's a little too late. That—whatever it was between us— is over and done."

She heard her father's tentative footsteps across the wood floor, followed by a gentle hand on her shoulder. "What happened?"

With a sigh, Morgan flipped the lid of her suitcase closed and flopped down onto the bed next to it. "He found out about Dawn." She dropped her face into her hands and felt the tears she'd been fighting back all day finally breaking free.

"Oh, sunshine." She felt the bed sink beside her as her father sat down and wrapped his arm around her.

"He was so angry that I'd kept it from him. He said that even if I *had* believed he extorted money from you to let the annulment go through, it hadn't been right to keep the pregnancy from him. Especially when I lost her. And he was right. River had a right to know. But this family is so damn worried about appearances. All the secrets and the lies…your lies…just weave a web so complex we can't help but get caught up in it."

She felt her father stiffen beside her. Perhaps he felt guilty. He should. Part of this was a mess of his making. Not all of it, but enough. Morgan had done her part by going along with it and keeping quiet. Over the last few days, since River walked away, she'd done a lot of thinking. Some about River and some about the lies and secrets he despised so much. He was right when he said it wasn't healthy to keep things bottled up like that. Morgan would rather have a scandal than live her life walking on eggshells, waiting for something to be uncovered.

"He was right. And I'm not going to lie anymore, Daddy. Hiding it doesn't make it hurt any less and I'm not going to pretend like none of that ever happened. I'm going to have Dawn moved to a real cemetery so she isn't hidden away from the world. I might even start a charity in her name to raise money for NICU facilities that care for premature babies. Since I'm done with Steele Tools, I think that's going to be my next move. With the latest equipment and research, maybe I can keep someone else from losing their child the way I lost mine."

There was a long silence. Morgan sat, waiting for her father to protest. To explain why that wasn't a good idea and how he just wanted to protect her. "Morgan..." he said at last, hesitating for a moment.

"I'm sorry if you feel like this will hurt the family or the company image, but I'm doing it. You can always bring up that I'm not really your daughter if that makes it easier on everyone."

"Morgan!" he shouted this time, turning to look at her with a stern expression he seldom, if ever, used with her. "Don't you ever say anything like that, *do you hear me*? You are my daughter. You are every bit my child, regardless of what a DNA test or anyone else says. It doesn't matter whether you're getting into trouble or the perfect angel you've always strived to be. It never has."

The words were said powerfully and they struck Morgan with the impact she needed. She'd always fought to be the child she thought her parents wanted. Since the DNA results had come back, she'd wondered if maybe the real Morgan Steele would've been more like the daughter her parents had hoped for. She wished she'd known that she had been loved as-is all this time. It would've saved her a lot of stress and heartache over the years. "Really?"

"Absolutely." He sighed and looked down at the floor. "You're my little girl. Since the day I held you in my arms, I've done everything I could to try and protect you from the world. I realize now that I made some wrong choices along the way and may even have made some situations worse. I'm not perfect. And I know now that I can't protect you from everything. You have to live your own life and make your own decisions. I'm sorry it took me so long to figure that out."

Morgan leaned against her father's shoulder. She knew that he loved her and just wanted what was best for her. Perhaps now they could move forward with a better understanding. There was no way to go back in time and fix what had already gone wrong.

"And if you're willing to stay around for a few more days, we can talk to my lawyers about setting up that charity for Dawn. I think it's a brilliant idea," he said. "And as soon as it's ready and operational, just tell me and I'll be the first to write a check. No more secrets."

Greg stared at his handcuffed wrists as they rested on the interrogation room table and frowned. He'd made a lot of plans, but he hadn't really firmed up a getaway strategy. He thought that in the chaos he would be able to slip away. He regretted that now.

Nothing had gone to plan. Not really. The second charge on the right side of the space hadn't detonated. If it had, it might've concealed his getaway better, but instead, he had just stood there, hitting the button again and again in frustration, but nothing happened. By the time he'd tossed the controller aside and made his way for the back door, someone must have spotted him.

A big hulking, angry someone he now recognized as Harley Dalton. The same guy whose girlfriend they'd kidnapped and ransomed for ten million only a few months before.

His ears were still ringing from the explosion, but he could hear the sound of someone's footsteps coming quick behind him. Before he could make it to his car, he felt a large hand clamp onto his collar and the next thing he knew, he was facedown in the dirt. It only took one strike to knock him unconscious and he'd woken up in the back of a cop car.

Greg glanced up at the mirror and the men who were no doubt watching him through the glass. He wouldn't get away with it this time. They'd get his prints off the detonator he'd carelessly discarded. With Dalton working the other case, they'd likely tie him to the kidnapping and maybe even the baby-swapping plot. He was screwed, and this time he had no one to blame but himself.

A moment later, the door opened and Harley stepped in with another detective beside him. Dalton had a bandaged cut on his forehead, probably from the explosion. It only served to make his angry scowl look all the more dangerous.

"Good morning, Greg. Can we get you some coffee or water or something?" the detective asked.

He shook his head. He wasn't about to give up some DNA or let his bladder get the best of him. He'd seen enough cop dramas to know how that worked.

"We found your second bomb in the ballroom. The work was so shoddy the bomb squad couldn't even set it off when they tried. I'm surprised the first one worked at all. You're lucky, though. If they'd both gone off, someone might've been seriously hurt or killed. Then you'd be looking at murder on top of everything else."

All that and the Steeles had walked away without much more than a few scratches on them. It figured. They were untouchable.

"Thanks to the legwork done by Mr. Dalton here, we've been able to link you back to not only the bomb but the recent kidnapping of Jade Nolan and the attempted abduction of Jade nearly thirty years ago. You've been a busy guy."

Dalton leaned back against the wall and crossed

his arms over his chest. It was no wonder Greg had been knocked out with one punch from those massive fists. "What happened, Greg?" he asked. "From the looks of it, you haven't been living the high life we expected. You got ten million dollars in ransom money from me and you've got nothing to show for it. No job, no money. It looks like you're living with your elderly father. That must've made you angry, to be your age and still living with your dad."

Greg didn't respond to the bait. It wouldn't help. He wasn't sure much would help him now, but he'd lean on the right to remain silent as long as he could.

The detective sat down at the table and leaned forward onto his elbows. "So what happened to all that money, Greg? Or should I ask, where's Buster and all that money?"

At that, Greg snorted in derision. "If I knew where Buster was, I would be there, getting my half out of him and pounding his smug-ass face for screwing me over."

Dalton rolled his eyes at Greg and the detective started writing things down. That was when Greg realized what he'd just said. So much for remaining silent. That's why Buster was the brains of the operation and Greg was in handcuffs.

"I want a lawyer," he said before he could make the situation any worse. "And I want a deal," he added. If he was going down, he sure as hell was taking Buster down with him.

River sat back in his chair and stared at the plans he was submitting as part of his company's bid for a big-city project. It was one of those new mixed-use developments, where retail, entertainment, dining, office spaces and housing all coexisted. The suburbs were an ideal of generations past. Millennials were more interested in living on a smaller scale in the middle of the action, spawning urban renewal projects all over the country.

This was a huge project and if Southern Charm got it, it would cement River's company in the Charleston real estate and development market. That's what the whole charity undertaking with Steele Tools had been about after all—raising visibility so he could land lucrative jobs like this.

At least that's what he told himself. River dropped the plans back onto his desk and sighed. If he were honest with himself, he knew it had had more to do with seeing Morgan again. Forcing her to look him in the eye and deal with what she'd done to him. To show her and her father that he wasn't the lost cause they'd believed him to be. That hadn't exactly gone the way he'd anticipated. It had gone far, far better. Until it fell apart.

"Mr. Atkinson, there's a Mr. Steele here to see you."

River frowned at his phone. His heart had leaped for a moment at the name Steele, thinking perhaps it was Morgan. But no. It was probably one of her brothers coming by to drop off something inconsequential.

"Send him in," he responded. River quickly rolled up the plans he was going over and set them out of the way. When he looked up again, he was stunned to find it was the CEO, Trevor, not one of his sons, paying him a visit.

River stood up like a shot and straightened his tie. "I wasn't expecting you, Mr. Steele." The man crossed the room and reached out to shake River's hand for the first time. He was stunned into taking it and offering the man a seat. "Have a seat. What can I do for you, Mr. Steele?"

"Please," he insisted as he lowered himself into the chair. "Just call me Trevor. I'm not here on official company business today."

River tried to temper his surprise. Why else would this man be here? By all accounts, he hated River and would sooner have a restraining order put on him than smile in his direction. "Okay. To what do I owe this visit then?"

"I had a disturbing discussion with my daughter this morning and it made me realize that I needed to talk to you."

What disturbing things had she told her father to

send him across town to see River? Yes, they'd had a fight and he'd walked away, but what did that have to do with Trevor? "I don't understand."

The older man nodded and leaned forward to lightly wring his hands together as he gathered his thoughts. "She told me that you two broke up after the party. That you found out about Dawn." He shook his head. "This is all my fault," he added abruptly.

River hadn't been expecting that. Sure, he might blame the man for the role he had played, but he never imagined Trevor would agree with him. "Sir?"

"Everything that has gone wrong between the two of you. Dawn. I had a hand in most of it and I wanted to make sure you knew that. Don't blame Morgan." Trevor hesitated for a moment. "I want to tell you something. Something I've never told anyone before."

River sat up straight in his chair. He wasn't sure what Morgan's father was about to tell him, or if it would change anything between him and Morgan, but he was curious to hear what he had to say.

"I've never believed that Morgan was my daughter," he said. "Long before the DNA tests and news that the babies were switched in the hospital, I knew she wasn't mine. She didn't look like me or any of our other children. Naturally, I believed Patricia had taken a lover at some point."

River's breath froze in his lungs. He wasn't quite

sure if he was really hearing a confession like this from Trevor. It seemed too out of sync with what he knew of the man. But it made him sit at attention and listen because it likely wasn't going to happen again.

Trevor shook his head. "I tried to distance myself from the baby once I realized the truth. But it didn't take me long to fall head over heels for that little girl. Before she could walk, she had me wrapped around her pinky finger. I love my sons—don't get me wrong—but Morgan was and is my world. And over time, as she grew older and her appearance became more strikingly different from the rest of the family, I started to worry."

"That people would gossip about the affair?"

"No." Trevor gave him a pointed look of irritation that made River decide to keep his mouth shut until the man had finished whatever it was he had to say.

"To my knowledge, no one has ever publicly or privately questioned Morgan's paternity. But I began to worry that someday her biological father might show up and try to take her away from me. I was paralyzed by the fear of losing my baby girl to some mystery man with dark hair and green eyes. So I sheltered her. I protected Morgan to the point of smothering her to keep her safe and by my side. That was all I could think to do. And then one day, when I least expected it, a man did come into her life and I almost lost her."

Trevor looked up at River and smiled ruefully. "She had finally been stolen from me, but not in a way I ever expected. You came out of nowhere, and suddenly my baby girl was gone. I panicked when I heard the news that you two had eloped. I acted on reflex and I made some bad choices, trying to fix what I felt was a problem. It never once occurred to me that my baby girl wasn't a baby anymore, and it wasn't my mistake to correct.

"Everything that happened after that was me trying to shield her from being hurt, but it just made things worse. In an ironic twist, I drove her away by fighting to keep her close. Things were never the same between us."

Trevor sighed heavily and sat back in his chair. "And now, when I think about Dawn…and I try to put myself in your shoes as the baby's father… Considering how much I love Morgan, how would it feel to find out I'd lost a daughter I never knew about? One I never got to hold, to see or to mourn when she was gone. I would be devastated, no doubt. And angry that someone had robbed me of my chance. So I understand why you left."

He looked River in the eyes. "But I want you to be angry with me, not Morgan. Every secret she kept, every lie she told was because of me."

"It's not as simple as that, Mr. St—*Trevor*. I mean, yes, I was angry to learn she'd kept all that from me, but there's more to it than that."

"I understand. Relationships are difficult. Patricia and I have had our ups and downs over the last forty years, and the two of you have had plenty of challenges without my help. But you need to know that it's worth it. She's worth it. Worth the risk. Worth protecting. Worth sacrificing. She's worth it all, River."

River knew that. He wouldn't keep beating his head against this wall if being with her didn't make up for the pain. But how much would he have to sacrifice to have her in his life? He'd already lived the last few weeks in the shadows as they hid their relationship. He wasn't willing to do that anymore and he hoped he wouldn't have to. Trevor knew something was going on between them or he wouldn't be here. If they could be together in the open, that would be one less issue, but there were more. "I'm not sure what's going to happen with Morgan and me. There's a lot for me to think about."

"Of course. It can be scary to love someone that much. After all these years, all the things I've done to protect Morgan, I'm still scared of losing her. When the truth came out and I knew for certain she wasn't my biological child, I was petrified. I should've been relieved that my wife hadn't had an affair, but I wasn't. It was just confirmation of what I'd always known and feared—only now there was no blood tie to hold her here if she wanted to go to her real family. I wouldn't have blamed her. Everything I've done was more likely to drive her away than keep her here.

"But she didn't go. Even after everything. Even after knowing you two had split up again and it was my fault, she still looks at me with love in her eyes and calls me Daddy. I've been a fool and I'm sorry for what I've done to you out of my own misplaced fears."

River had done his best to keep up with the conversation, but it was a lot to take in. Trevor Steele had just laid his soul bare and apologized to him in a way he had never expected or anticipated. He hardly knew what to do or say to Morgan's father after something like this. "I don't know what to say," he voiced his worry aloud.

Trevor nodded softly. "I understand. Tell me this—do you love my daughter?"

Despite his anger and feelings of betrayal, that was an easy answer to give. "Yes, sir."

"Good. More than anything, I want Morgan to be happy. You made her happy then, and you make her happy now, River. I know that I've shown up here and dumped a lot of my baggage on you, but there's a good reason for it. Today, I saw my little girl more brokenhearted than I've seen her in a long time. I can't fix the hurts of the past that I've caused, but it's not too late to do something now. I came here today in the hopes that I could explain myself to you and perhaps you wouldn't let my mistakes ruin your future together."

The older man's words seemed to stir something inside of him. Perhaps he was right.

"She's agreed to stay in town for another week to handle some legal matters. Go to her and tell her how you feel," Trevor said. "And if she loves you half as much as I think she does, this time, don't let me or anyone else get in the way of you two being together."

Twelve

"Your birthday is coming up soon."

Jade looked up from her phone as Harley came into the room. He had a satisfied smirk on his face as he leaned in and gave her a hello kiss. "Thanks for the reminder."

"Thirty is a big birthday. We need to do something."

"Like what?"

Harley reached into his suit coat breast pocket and pulled out a check. He handed it over to her. "Whatever you want. I've got my payment from St. Francis Hospital burning a hole in my pocket."

Jade's eyes grew wide when she saw the digits on

the check. Even more so, she was excited about what the check meant. If the hospital had paid Harley, the job he had been originally hired for—to find out who switched Jade with another child at St. Francis—was done at last. "It's over?"

"It's over, baby."

Jade stood up and leaped into Harley's arms. "Tell me everything!"

He hugged her tight, then led her over to the couch. "After we arrested Greg Crowley for the bombing, he was anxious to cut a deal. He spilled on everything, from the baby switch, to the kidnapping, to finally the bombing. The maternity nurse was his sister, Nancy, and when she committed suicide, she did so without telling Greg and her boyfriend, Buster, where the Steeles' daughter ended up. They didn't know where you were until you went on the news almost thirty years later. They decided that was their chance to get their payoff, and it worked."

"So why did Greg turn around and blow up the Steele mansion? I would've taken the ten million and disappeared."

"He was angry. Buster screwed him and took all the money, disappearing. Greg was out for revenge and targeted the Steele family because he decided they were the cause of all his troubles. Thanks to some superior detective work on my team's part, we were able to track Buster down to Honduras. He was extradited back to the US on Wednesday and is being held without bail until his trial."

"Wow." Jade sat back against the soft couch cushions and tried to absorb everything he'd told her. It had been over six months since she'd first gotten her DNA results and the world had been turned on its ear. To know the truth finally, and for the men responsible to be in jail where they belonged, was a huge weight off her shoulders.

"When they found Buster, they also found his stash of money. The idiot was keeping all that cash in the same duffel bag I used to leave the ransom money. He'd only spent about fifty grand, so Trevor and I got most of it back."

Jade let out an audible sigh of relief. She'd never said anything to Harley or Trevor, but she'd felt horribly guilty about the money they'd paid for her ransom. When the cops failed to catch them, it was like ten million dollars had vanished into thin air. Getting it back was almost as big of a relief as the men being arrested.

"So I was thinking…since I got all that money back, we should do something good with it. Not just for your birthday, but maybe we could look into some real estate here. Like a house."

"A house here?" She perked up in surprise. They'd been so focused on the investigation that they'd never really discussed what they would do after it was done. She'd presumed they would go to DC eventually, but any talks about where they would live, when they would marry... It had all been pushed to the future. Apparently, the future had arrived without warning and she wasn't at all prepared.

"Yes, here. You love it in Charleston. I really can't see you living anywhere else."

"I do like it here, but I can work anywhere. Your business is based out of DC. That's more important."

"And it's run perfectly fine the last six months with me here. Isaiah has managed, but if we stay here, I'll get someone to run the business for me full time. I've never enjoyed that part of the work. And maybe I'll get a small plane I can use to fly back and forth when I need to."

Jade couldn't keep her jaw from dropping. She didn't really want to move away from her family, old and new, but she was willing to do whatever she had to for Harley. She had never expected him to be willing to do the same for her. "Really?"

Harley moved closer and pulled Jade into his arms. "Anything you want, my love. With all this behind us, we can start our lives together without the shadow hanging over our heads. No one is ever going to hurt you again, and I'm going to spend every day of my life making you smile."

River looked down at the ring the jeweler held out to him. It had taken three days to get it ready, but it was finally done. The jeweler probably thought he was crazy, having two round flawless pink diamonds added to such a cheap diamond ring. It was ten-karat gold plated with a diamond that would require a magnifying glass to see if not for the thick mounting making it look larger. It was all his twenty-one-year-old self had been able to afford.

Morgan had never looked at the ring with anything less than beaming enthusiasm. She'd told him that she was rich and could have all the diamonds she could want, but one given to her by River was more special than anything else.

He'd kept that thought in mind after Trevor left that afternoon. A lot had gone through his mind as he tried to process everything he'd just been told. By the time he lay down in bed that night, he realized that he'd been too harsh on Morgan. In the moment, it had felt like the ultimate betrayal, and maybe it was, but he had to understand her side of the story, too.

Married or not, they had been just kids. And to find herself pregnant and scared—believing only the worst about River—she'd done what she had to do and kept it a secret from him. Then she had to go through a scary delivery and the loss of their daughter alone. He couldn't imagine what that had to have been like for her. She lost her love and her child, and was put in a position by her family not to be able to talk about it to anyone.

The thought made River's stomach ache. But by morning, he knew what he had to do to put everything right. That meant going to Morgan and winning her over for good. Not dating, not just some fling, but a real relationship. Another chance at their marriage.

He'd considered buying another engagement ring. It wouldn't be hard to find a nicer, flashier one with a fat, flawless diamond set in platinum. He could afford it now. But there was something about this old one that seemed special enough to keep, so he'd dug it out of his sock drawer and taken it to the jeweler for some upgrades.

With the work finished, he admired the ring and wrapped up the transaction. River accepted the tiny gift bag from the jeweler and walked out of the shop with nervous anticipation. He wasn't unfamiliar with the concept of proposing to a woman. He'd done it once, and successfully. He'd even proposed to the same woman. But this time was very different.

That Morgan had been head over heels for him and hadn't had a worry in the world. Love was everything she needed. That young naïve girl would learn soon after her engagement how hard life could be on her heart. The Morgan he was heading to see now had lived ten more years. She'd experienced more heartbreak and loss than someone her age should.

Some of that was his fault. And that was why he wasn't so sure how this was going to go. Her father seemed positive that she cared for him, but would she opt for self-preservation over her feelings? He wouldn't blame her if she did.

Climbing into his truck, he set the ring on the passenger seat and started driving to Mount Pleasant. Whether or not he would be successful, it had to be tonight. Trevor had called that morning to tell him that the legal matters had been handled more quickly than he'd expected and Morgan was driving back to DC in the morning. He also mentioned that he and his wife would be out to dinner after six o'clock with Morgan alone at the house.

It wasn't subtle, but River appreciated what the man was trying to do. Tonight was the night. And if he failed, she was gone tomorrow.

True, Washington, DC, wasn't the other side of the world, but it wasn't Savannah, either, and her ties to Charleston grew more tenuous as time went on. She had told him about how she'd quit her job at Steele Tools. He wasn't sure what she intended to do now, but if she took a job somewhere else, she could be on the west coast before he could try to change her mind.

After everything that had happened over the last few weeks, he got the feeling that Morgan wouldn't be coming back to Charleston for a very long time.

The windows of the Steele mansion were mostly dark as he pulled in. He could see her Mercedes convertible parked on the far side of the motor court, so he knew she was home. He parked by the front door and slipped the ring box into his pocket before getting out.

It felt a bit surreal coming back to the house after everything that had happened the night of the key ceremony. But he climbed up the steps anyway and rang the doorbell.

It took several minutes, but eventually he heard footsteps clicking across the marble foyer floor. River was expecting the housekeeper to answer, but when the door swung open, he found a stunned Morgan standing there instead.

Her mouth was agape, but after a moment, she clamped her lips shut and narrowed her gaze. Her expression hardened, her face regarding him with more distaste than it had when he'd first shown up in the ballroom. "What are you doing here, River?"

That was an icier reception than even he had been expecting. He was the one who had been lied to, but he'd obviously hurt her as well with how he'd handled the whole situation. Taking a deep breath, he told himself to go for it anyway. The thorniest fruits held the sweetest juices. "I wanted to talk to you."

Morgan crossed her arms over her chest, protectively. "Well, I don't want to talk to you. When I tried to explain myself, you weren't interested in listening to what I had to say. You just wanted to yell and blame me, and I've had my fill of that for the week."

"I'm interested in listening now. And I'm sorry for how I reacted. You have no idea how sorry. I just needed some time to think. We've both made mistakes, Morgan. Then and now. Please let me in so we can talk. I don't want to do this on the front porch, but I will."

Her green eyes searched his face for a moment, then she acquiesced and took a step back from the door. "Come in," she said, although her tone was anything but welcoming.

River stepped inside and glanced over at the ballroom. There was still police tape and plastic tarps blocking most of the view, but he could see some late evening light coming through the hole left by the man's bomb. Morgan ignored the mess and led him to the west side of the mansion that was untouched by the explosion.

She opened a pair of double wooden doors that led into the library. The scent of leather and old books assaulted his senses as they stepped inside. Morgan approached the hunter green leather sofa with ornate dark wood details and sat at one end, indicating he should do the same.

"I overreacted when I learned about Dawn," he started out, but Morgan held up her hand to stop him.

"No. No, you didn't. You reacted exactly the way a man would react to news like that. That's why I dreaded telling you the truth. I didn't want to ruin what we had, but I knew we couldn't be together if I couldn't be honest. Did I tell you now or horde as many minutes and hours with you as I could before the truth came out? I backed myself into a corner and there was no way out of it. The moment I realized where we were in the gardens, I knew it was all over."

River reached out and took Morgan's hand. "It's not over. Not by a long shot."

She looked at her hand in his and back up at him. "It is, River. We have too much baggage weighing us down. Too many secrets and too much hurt. Eventually, no matter how hard we fight to stay afloat, it's going to pull us under. I will always have the scars on my body that Dawn's birth left behind. Every time I see them, every time you see them, the past will come back to haunt us."

River squeezed his eyes shut tight as the pieces started coming together at last. "That's what you were hiding from me," he said.

Morgan nodded. "I wish it were just a bad tattoo. But the scar... I knew if you saw it, you would have questions. It's a physical reminder of the pain I went through, but even harder to ignore than the psychological scars. You might think that you've forgiven me or my family for what happened, but that kind of wound never really heals completely."

"That's not true."

"It is true. I tell myself that it has to be to protect what's left of my fragile spirit. River, don't ask me to give my heart to you, because every time I do it, I get it back in pieces. Don't make promises about our future and how everything will be okay, because one day when I least expect it, you're going to change your mind and realize you can't forgive me. I can't go through that. I'd rather walk away now and safeguard myself than give in and get hurt again."

"Do you think that I haven't been hurt just as badly? I have. The woman I loved was taken from me for no other reason than I wasn't good enough for her. Our love wasn't allowed to exist because I was poor and uneducated. It was my all-time low point. After I lost you, the idea of starting and building my new company was the only thing getting me out of bed every day. I wanted to make myself better so something like that never happened to me again. If I'm being honest with myself, I wanted to make myself worthy of being the husband your father wanted for you. I didn't believe I stood a chance at winning you again, but I had to try. It was that or give up on everything."

Morgan bit at her lip, her eyes starting to shimmer with the first flicker of emotion. "River, I'm scared."

Moving over to her, River scooped her into his arms. She wrapped herself around him just as tightly, burying her face in his neck. With his lips against the outer shell of her ear, he whispered, "I'm scared, too. I can't promise you that you'll never get hurt. That's impossible. I can't promise you that I won't ever say or do something that upsets you. Or that we won't make mistakes. Couples fight. They argue. But if they love each other and fight for that love, they'll make it through. We've had a rocky start, but I intend to make it to the finish line with you by my side, Morgan."

River pulled away to look her in the eye. "You're worth the risk. You always have been, to me."

Reaching into his pocket, he pulled out the ring. He slipped off the couch onto one knee and opened the box on its hinge. He offered it up to Morgan and held his breath. It was now or never.

Thirty minutes ago, Morgan was putting a few last things in her luggage and pondering what time she was leaving in the morning. Lena had just pestered her about coming downstairs for some dinner, but she wasn't in the mood to eat. Really, she had lost her appetite the night of the key ceremony. Every time she tried to eat, her throat tried to close up on her. She supposed that was better than drowning her sorrow in cookies.

Then the doorbell had rung. Morgan was in the laundry, looking for her favorite blouse, when she heard it. Lena had her hands full with a load of towels she was pulling from the dryer, so Morgan had gone to answer the door.

She wasn't sure who she had been expecting to be there. The police had come and gone for a while, and then the press had been a nuisance, investigating the bombing for the papers, but that had tapered off. She never could've anticipated what the ringing of the doorbell would bring into her life.

"We've already lost years together because of other people's expectations and demands. I would give anything to go back in time and throw that check in your father's face. Even if just so I could be there to hold your hand when we lost our daughter. But I can't do anything about that and neither can you. What's done is done. All I know now is that I love you. I've always loved you, Morgan. And I can't bear the idea of losing any more time with you. I want our future together to start right now, if you'll have me."

Morgan's heart was pounding so loudly in her chest she could barely hear River's heartfelt words. She had to focus intently on each sentence, but it was difficult when he opened the ring box and blew her away. Not because he was proposing—which was a surprise in and of itself—but because of the ring he held up to her.

It was *her* ring.

She stared at it for a moment before she realized it, because the ring wasn't exactly as she remembered. She reached out and plucked it from its velvet bed to study the inside of the band and the words she knew would be there.

You are my everything, it read. Just as it had all those years ago. It was her original engagement ring. With a few notable enhancements.

She didn't know what to say. When she realized what was happening, she'd expected a big gaudy ring. He was a man of means now, so it was practically a given that he would buy a new diamond to propose to her. But he hadn't. He'd given her back the ring he'd chosen for her all those years ago.

"This is *my* ring," she whispered in disbelief. He could've spent any amount of money on a ring, but he was offering her the one he had given her the first time. The one he'd saved months for, eating nothing but ramen noodles and peanut butter to afford. That meant more than any of the flashy gems she'd spied on the hands of local society ladies at the charity gala.

River nodded. "It is."

"How did you...?" She looked down at him, still

on his knee, with her eyes blurring with tears. "You kept the ring all this time?"

"I did. When you sent it back to me, I didn't have the heart to get rid of it. For a few years, I even carried it around in my wallet as a reminder."

"A reminder of how much I hurt you?"

"No. Of how much you loved me. And then I finally put it away in a drawer, but I never forgot it was there. After our fight, I did some thinking and I decided it was time to put it to good use again. It's been gathering dust for too long."

The tears were flowing in earnest now. "You changed it since I saw it last." It was a stupid observation in the moment, but she couldn't think of anything else. She was overwhelmed with so many feelings she could hardly figure out how to process everything. All she could do was focus on the two shining pink stones on each side of her original diamond. They were beautifully cut trillion stones, enhancing the center setting without managing to overpower it. It reminded her of the pink diamond at the Smithsonian. The one she'd told River she loved.

"I did. I had the jeweler add two pink diamonds to it. For Dawn."

Morgan clutched the ring in her fist and held it against her chest as her heart swelled with emotions. This was the most precious thing he could ever give her. It was a sign, an undeniable one, that what they had in their youth was real, not just some puppy love. If this symbol of their love, and now a symbol of their daughter, could survive all these years, they could, too.

Taking a breath, she wiped the tears from her cheeks and slipped the ring onto her finger. She admired it for a moment before she said, "Yes."

River looked up from admiring the ring on her hand with confusion lining his eyes. "Yes, what?"

She smiled. They'd discussed the details of the ring for so long, her acceptance of his proposal was out of context. She reached out and took his hands into hers. "Yes, I will marry you, River Atkinson."

He leaped to his feet and pulled Morgan up from the couch with him. She fell into his arms, wrapping her own around his neck to pull his lips to hers.

Yes, she would marry him. And this time, it would be forever.

Epilogue

Nine months later, you'd never know that a bomb had ripped through the Steele mansion. It was pristinely restored and ready for Morgan and River's big day.

Like their first time around, they'd chosen a warm Saturday in the summer. This time, as Morgan walked down the aisle, it was in a Vera Wang gown, with hair and makeup done by professionals and a gorgeous bouquet of peach roses and white lilies in her hands. Both Trevor and Arthur Nolan walked her down the rose petal–strewn lawn, one on each arm.

She'd spent a lot of time getting to know her new family once she'd opted to stay in Charleston permanently with River. When wedding plans had turned to the bride's family and their roles in the ceremony, she'd known exactly what she wanted to do. Both her mothers were beaming from the front row with their corsages, and both fathers were teary as they gave her away. The Nolans had been excited and pleased to be included on Morgan's big day.

It was hard for Morgan to compare this wedding day to the last one. Instead of just the two of them at a rustic mountain chapel, they were at her family home surrounded by hundreds of familiar faces. All their friends and family were there to see the big event.

The day was glorious, splendid, but filled with no more love than it had been at their first ceremony. Her eyes filled with tears as she recited her vows for the second time, just as they had originally. And when they kissed, her heart leaped in her chest, knowing that she would be with the man she loved forever now. No secrets. No more sneaking around.

No one in the audience was more pleased or smiling more brightly than Jade. After finding out everything her sister had been through just because of the life she'd been placed into, she was so glad to see her happy with the man she loved. Even then, about halfway through the reception, she leaned over to Harley and whispered into his ear, "This is nice and all, but when we get married…"

He held up his hand to stop her. "I vote that we elope under a waterfall in Hawaii and spend our wedding budget on a month-long honeymoon in Bora Bora. We can get one of those thatched roof huts over the water and eat seafood until we're sick at the sight of it. I don't need this circus to make our love legally binding."

"Agreed. You read my mind." Jade smiled and took his hand in hers. They were a perfectly imperfect match.

"I'm that good," Harley said. Bringing his fingertips up to one temple, he closed his eyes in concentration. "I'm also sensing that you would like to dance." He pushed back his chair and offered his hand to help Jade up.

She accepted and followed him out to the dance floor. A romantic slow song was being played by the orchestra and quite a few people were already out there. The bride and groom were sharing a moment, as were Trevor and Patricia, and Carolyn and Arthur. Jade was happy to see her whole family had been included on Morgan's big day. Their situation was complicated, but they were working hard on being one big confusing family.

As Jade slipped happily into Harley's large, strong arms, she noticed one of her new brothers dancing nearby with a beautiful blonde. It was one of the twins, and she was ashamed to admit she still wasn't able to tell Sawyer and Finn apart.

"You skeevy little prick!"

The angry shout cut through the sounds in the ballroom like a knife. The dancers paused, and even the orchestra was startled into silence. Everyone turned to see the stunning redhead standing at the edge of the dance floor. Her hair was as fiery as her temper and it was focused directly on the twin who was dancing nearby.

"Who is that woman, Sawyer?" the blonde dancing with him asked.

Sawyer shook his head. "I have no idea. Can I help you?"

"Can you help me?" she repeated bitterly. "Yes. You can hold still." The angry woman walked up to Sawyer and slapped him hard across the face. There was a collective gasp as everyone in the ballroom froze, waiting to see what was going to happen next.

Two of Harley's brawniest security guys intervened before things could escalate. As quietly and discreetly as they could, they whispered into the woman's ear and escorted her out of the ballroom. A moment later, Sawyer went after the redhead, leaving his date looking confused and annoyed on the dance floor.

"I wonder what that was all about," Jade said as the music started up again.

"With this family? I couldn't even begin to guess!" Harley laughed. "All I know is that we're definitely eloping and going to Bora Bora."

* * * * *

*What's going on with the Steele twins?
Don't miss Sawyer's book,
coming in 2020!*

Get 4 FREE REWARDS!

We'll send you 2 FREE Books plus 2 FREE Mystery Gifts.

YES! Please send me 2 FREE Harlequin® Desire novels and my 2 FREE gifts (gifts are worth about $10 retail). After receiving them, if I don't wish to receive any more books, I can return the shipping statement marked "cancel." If I don't cancel, I will receive 6 brand-new novels every month and be billed just $4.55 per book in the U.S. or $5.24 per book in Canada. That's a savings of at least 13% off the cover price! It's quite a bargain! Shipping and handling is just 50¢ per book in the U.S. and $1.25 per book in Canada.* I understand that accepting the 2 free books and gifts places me under no obligation to buy anything. I can always return a shipment and cancel at any time. The free books and gifts are mine to keep no matter what I decide.

225/326 HDN GNND

Name (please print)

Address   Apt. #

City   State/Province   Zip/Postal Code

Mail to the **Reader Service**:
IN U.S.A.: P.O. Box 1341, Buffalo, NY 14240-8531
IN CANADA: P.O. Box 603, Fort Erie, Ontario L2A 5X3

Want to try 2 free books from another series? Call 1-800-873-8635 or visit www.ReaderService.com.

SPECIAL EXCERPT FROM

H
HQN™

*For Vanessa Logan, returning home was about healing,
not exploring her attraction to cowboy Jacob Dalton!
But walking away from their explosive chemistry is
proving impossible…*

Read on for a sneak preview of
Lone Wolf Cowboy *by* New York Times *and*
USA TODAY *bestselling author Maisey Yates.*

She curled her hands into fists, grabbing hold of his T-shirt.
And she had no idea what the hell was running through her
head as she stood there looking up into those wildly blue
eyes, the present moment mingling with memories of that
night long ago.

While he witnessed the deepest, darkest thing she'd ever
gone through. Something no one else even knew about.

He was the only one who knew.

The only one who knew what had started everything.
Olivia didn't understand. Her parents didn't understand.
And they had never wanted to understand.

But he knew. He knew and he had already seen what a
disaster she was.

There was no facade to protect. No new enlightened
sense of who she was. No narrative about her as a lost cause
out there roaming the world.

He'd already seen her break apart. For real. Not the
Vanessa that existed when she was hiding. Hiding her
problems from her family. Hiding her feelings behind a high.

Hiding. And more hiding.

No. He had seen her at her lowest when she hadn't been able to hide.

And somehow, he seemed to bring that out in her. Because she wasn't able to hide her anger.

And she wasn't able to hide this. Whatever the wildness was that was coursing through her veins. No, she couldn't hide that either. And she wasn't sure she cared.

So she was just going to let the wildness carry her forward.

She couldn't remember the last time she had done that. The last time she'd allowed herself this pure kind of over-the-top emotion.

It had been pain. The pain she felt that night she lost the baby. That was the last time she had let it all go. In all the time since then when she had been on the verge of being overwhelmed by emotion she had crushed it completely. Hidden it beneath drugs. Hidden it beneath therapy speak.

She had carefully kept herself in hand since she'd gotten sober. Kept herself under control.

What she hadn't allowed herself to do was feel.

She was feeling now. And she wasn't going to stop it.

She launched herself forward, and her lips connected with his.

And before she knew it, she was kissing Jacob Dalton with all the passion she hadn't known existed inside of her.

Don't miss
Lone Wolf Cowboy *by Maisey Yates,*
available August 2019 wherever
Harlequin® books and ebooks are sold.

www.Harlequin.com

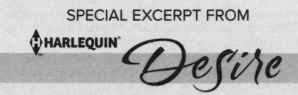
"To answer your other question," he murmured. "Why did I
single you out? Your first guess was correct. Because you are
so beautiful I couldn't help following you around this over-
the-top ballroom filled with people who possess more money
than sense. The women here can't outshine you. They're like
peacocks, spreading their plumage, desperate to be noticed,
and here you are among them, like the moon. Bright, alone,
above it all and eclipsing every one of them. What I don't
understand is how no one else noticed before me. Why every
man in this place isn't standing behind me in a line just for
the chance to be near you."

Silence swelled around them like a bubble, muting the din
of the gala. His words seemed to echo in the cocoon, and he
marveled at them. Hadn't he sworn he didn't do pretty words?
Yet it had been him talking about peacocks and moons.

What was she doing to him?

Even as the question echoed in his mind, her head tilted
back and she stared at him, her lovely eyes darker...hotter. In

that moment, he'd stand under a damn balcony and serenade her if she continued looking at him like that. He curled his fingers into his palm, reminding himself with the pain that he couldn't touch her. Still, the only sound that reached his ears was the quick, soft pants breaking on her pretty lips.

"I—I need to go," she whispered, already shifting back and away from him. "I—" She didn't finish the thought, but turned and waded into the crowd, distancing herself from him.

He didn't follow; she hadn't said no, but she hadn't said yes, either. And though he'd caught the desire in her gaze— his stomach still ached from the gut punch of it—she had to come to him.

Or ask him to come for her.

Rooted where she'd left him, he tracked her movements.

Saw the moment she cleared the mass of people and strode in the direction of the double doors where more tray-bearing staff emerged and exited.

Saw when she paused, palm pressed to one of the panels.

Saw when she glanced over her shoulder in his direction.

Even across the distance of the ballroom, the electric shock of that look whipped through him, sizzled in his veins. Moments later, she disappeared from view. Didn't matter; his feet were already moving in her direction.

That glance, that look. It'd sealed her fate.

Sealed it for both of them.

What will happen when these two find each other alone during the blackout?

Find out in
Black Tie Billionaire
by USA TODAY *bestselling author Naima Simone*
available September 2019 wherever
Harlequin® Desire books and ebooks are sold.

www.Harlequin.com

Want to give in to temptation with
steamy tales of irresistible desire?

Check out **Harlequin® Presents®**,
Harlequin® Desire and
Harlequin® Kimani™ Romance books!

New books available every month!

CONNECT WITH US AT:

Facebook.com/groups/HarlequinConnection

 Facebook.com/HarlequinBooks

 Twitter.com/HarlequinBooks

 Instagram.com/HarlequinBooks

Pinterest.com/HarlequinBooks

ReaderService.com

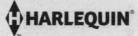

**ROMANCE WHEN
YOU NEED IT**

PGENRE2018

2431

Love Harlequin romance?

DISCOVER.

Be the first to find out about promotions,
news and exclusive content!

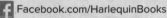 Facebook.com/HarlequinBooks

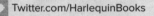 Twitter.com/HarlequinBooks

Instagram.com/HarlequinBooks

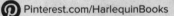 Pinterest.com/HarlequinBooks

ReaderService.com

EXPLORE.

Sign up for the Harlequin e-newsletter and
download a free book from any series at
TryHarlequin.com.

CONNECT.

Join our Harlequin community to share
your thoughts and connect with other
romance readers!
Facebook.com/groups/HarlequinConnection

 **HARLEQUIN**®

**ROMANCE WHEN
YOU NEED IT**